DUET IN LOW KEY

In their quiet Highland village, the minister, David Sinclair, and his wife Morag, await the return of their daughter Bridget from convalescence. But a newcomer to the village causes Morag some consternation. Ledoux, big and flamboyant, is a Canadian forester, and has caused a stir locally. Morag fears that Ledoux, at a loose end in the quiet community, might make a play for their gentle and innocent daughter — and the potential for scandal would never do . . .

DORIS RAE

---◆---

DUET IN LOW KEY

Complete and Unabridged

LINFORD
Leicester

First published in Great Britain in 1974 by
Robert Hale & Company
London

First Linford Edition
published 2008
by arrangement with
Robert Hale Limited
London

British Library CIP Data

Rae, Doris
    Duet in low key.—Large print ed.—
Linford romance library
1. Love stories
2. Large type books
I. Title
823.9′14 [F]

ISBN 978–1–84782–378–6

Published by
F. A. Thorpe (Publishing)
Anstey, Leicestershire

Set by Words & Graphics Ltd.
Anstey, Leicestershire
Printed and bound in Great Britain by
T. J. International Ltd., Padstow, Cornwall

This book is printed on acid-free paper

1

'Of course it just had to happen now.' Mrs Sinclair rested her basket on the counter and looked across at Mrs Macleod. 'I've just been in having a word with Hamish and he says there's a part he's needing. It'll take two days at least to get it.'

'Well now! That is vexing,' Mrs Macleod was sympathetic. 'And young Bridget coming home tomorrow you say?'

'Yes. Her aunt is seeing her on the train at Edinburgh and I'd planned to pick her up in Inverness and drive her out home. We thought it wouldn't be so tiring for her that way. Ah, well, it can't be helped. I'll just need to get on to them when I get back to the manse and tell Bridget she's to get the train through to Achnasheen and take the bus from there.'

1

'It is vexing,' Mrs Macleod said again. 'And the poor lassie just out of hospital. Was the minister going in with you, Mrs Sinclair?'

Morag Sinclair smiled as she shook her head. 'No. I was going to treat myself to a morning's shopping on my own before I met Bridget in the afternoon. That wretched car! And Mrs Murray went off on Thursday or else she'd have taken me in.'

'Aye. I did hear the doctor and Mrs Murray were away off on their holiday. Away over to the continent too!' Mrs Macleod broke off and looked over Mrs Sinclair's shoulder. 'Is it your magazines you're after, Mr Ledoux?' she asked.

The shop door had opened and shut a few minutes before but as no one who came into the store was ever in a hurry and a browse around the well-filled shelves was the accepted thing, neither woman had bothered to break off their conversation. Now Morag turned too and smiled and said a bright 'Good afternoon, Mr Ledoux,' to the young man who stepped forward to her side. But there was a brief flash of mingled amusement and disapproval in her eyes as she viewed him.

Mr Ledoux undoubtedly wore the gaudiest shirts she had ever seen. The vivid red and blue checks of today's effort had to be seen to be believed. David who in his younger days had had a liking for films about the far wild west had said they were typical lumberjacks' wear. The other men working for the Forestry Commission did seem to have a taste for bright colours but none of them could compete with the man in charge of their squad. Ledoux topped them all in another way too for he was a big man, a giant someone in the village had called him, well over six feet in height with broad shoulders but with narrow hips. He was a dark man, his black hair growing thickly to curl slightly at the nape of his neck, but trimmed neatly as it grew in front of his ears, where it served to emphasize the dark tan of his weathered skin, as did his black and thick eyebrows and the two inch scar down his left cheek. A big and virile and colourful young man who would not go unnoticed, Mrs Sinclair knew, but to her way of thinking rather too much so in every way to fit into their quiet village life even temporarily.

But the man was smiling at her and returning her greeting and whatever reservations Morag had about him, he had always been polite and pleasant when she had met him. 'Good afternoon, Mrs Sinclair. Yes, if you have them I'll take them, Mrs Macleod.' He looked at the other woman and then back to Morag. 'Mrs Sinclair, I've to take a trip to Inverness tomorrow, so I'll take you in and bring you out again if that would be a help.'

'It's kind of you to offer, Mr Ledoux,' Mrs Sinclair said hesitantly. Quickly she swallowed her dismay and went on brightly, 'But it's of no consequence. I couldn't think to trouble you.'

'No trouble at all, Mrs Sinclair,' the young man replied easily. 'My business will take me till after lunch, so if you've someone to meet off the train I'll pick you up at the station.'

An offer of help in such circumstances was usual in a country district such as theirs, and if it had come from anyone else Mrs Sinclair would have accepted without any thought. Even now if it had been only for herself she would have accepted though reluctantly. But there was Bridget. But before she could even begin to think of a tactful excuse, Mrs Macleod, magazines in hand, had turned back to the counter.

She was beaming. 'Now isn't that lucky for you, Mrs Sinclair. It's the minister's young daughter who is coming home tomorrow, Mr Ledoux,' she told the man. 'The poor lassie had been ill, and travelling all the way from Edinburgh to Inverness will be tiring enough for her, without stopping and starting all the rest of the way.'

5

Morag's mouth thinned but she knew she would have to accept now. Otherwise it would be all round the village that the minister's wife had snubbed young Ledoux. And David would not be pleased about that. In fact he would be very annoyed. And, of course, she would not want to do that herself, for she had nothing against the young man. If only she had not been meeting Bridget!

She smiled and gave a little graceful nod. 'Thank you, Mr Ledoux. It's good of you, I'm sure. What time will you be leaving in the morning?'

Ledoux passed some coins over the counter to Mrs Macleod and took his magazines with a smiling Thank you. 'About nine, Mrs Sinclair,' he said. 'Unless that is too early for you?'

'No, no, that'll be fine for me.'

'You'll be able to get your bit of shopping done after all, Mrs Sinclair,' Mrs Macleod was still beaming.

The young man smiled. 'I'll be at the manse at nine then, Mrs Sinclair.' He nodded to both women and went quickly from the shop.

Mrs Macleod chuckled. 'My, it was lucky he came in at that moment now, wasn't it?' She laughed. 'He's a fine strapping laddie. Makes you feel like a midget.'

'He does that,' Mrs Sinclair agreed. 'He's colourful too,' she added with a slight edge of acidity to her tone which passed unnoticed.

'Aye, he is,' Mrs Macleod's eyes twinkled. 'They do say he's playing havoc at the hotel. Mrs Robertson says they have all their unattached young girl visitors, and many of the attached ones too, absolutely drooling over him.'

And that, thought Morag Sinclair as she too left the store and turned up the long hill to where the hotel sat in its fine position looking out over the bay, was what was worrying her. It was most unfortunate that the Canadian, French-Canadian he was really, had had to come into the shop just in time to overhear her conversation with Mrs

Macleod. David, of course, would agree with Mrs Macleod and say it was lucky. David liked the young man, he had heard he was a good man at his job, and kept his men in order, young as he was. David, of course, had been pleased when Ledoux had appeared in the kirk each Sunday morning during the month he had been in the village. That had been a surprise for with his name and his nationality it might have been supposed that a Scottish kirk would have been the last place he would have entered. Probably, Morag had suggested, he was just at a loose end on a Sunday morning, but David would not agree with that.

It was not that she disliked young Ledoux Morag told herself. She might not approve of him, but she did not dislike him. Providing she could keep him at the required distance, she was quite prepared to greet him pleasantly and graciously when she met him. But to let him drive her all the way to Inverness, and to drive not only her, but

Bridget too, all the way back, would give him a degree of intimacy with their family which she had certainly never intended him to have. Most certainly not with Bridget. Not, of course, that he was the type of young man who would appeal to her youngest daughter at all, she thought complacently.

Ledoux was well in front of her now, his long light strides taking him quickly up the hill. Morag, coming more slowly up the long road, saw him turn into the hotel, that terrible shirt still in evidence even from this distance. She hoped he would put on something at least a little quieter for the trip to Inverness tomorrow.

She quickened her steps, hoping that David, whom she had left working in the garden as he always did on a Monday morning, had remembered to switch on the cooker. She waved to old Mrs Cameron, busy snipping her roses in front of one of the small white cottages on her left hand, but did not even look to her right hand, where the sea, the tide out now, was lapping gently against the stretch of yellow sand, the massing of black rocks. Beyond the sun was shining on the blue water, on the horizon the outline of the northern coast of Skye was unmistakable, the island of Lewis was a faint grey cloud to the far north. Behind Mrs Sinclair as she walked the road fell to the long white building which was the store, branching there to the main road climbing steeply up on to the rising moors, to a narrower lane curving with the bay, backed for a hundred yards or so by low white and grey cottages, then going on to edge the long sweep of the northern arm.

The scattered village was hardly a village at all, not even one long street, for from the few cottages and the store on the low ground to the hotel in its fine position on a neck of land overlooking the centre of the splendid bay was half a mile, and there was another half mile of curving road before it reached the bank house, set back from the road. A couple of hundred yards further on was the tiny church and the manse, again standing in isolation. Beyond that another quarter of a mile brought the post office and a few fishermen's cottages to mark the end of the village.

Morag reached the hotel with the garage beyond and slowed. Should she go again to see if she could prevail upon Hamish to try to get the necessary spare part from somewhere today. But it was useless and she knew it. In all the twenty odd years she had known him she had never known Hamish be hurried.

She went on again, the road dipping and rising to another viewpoint. A wide stretch of golden sand was framed by a curve of fresh green and lapped by the blue water. Secluded and some distance from hotel and houses it was the best place from which to bathe, and when the family had been at home at the manse they had made good use of it. Beyond were all the colours of the southern arm of land which curved round the bay and on this fine day there was a glow of colour about both land and sea. But Morag Sinclair, apart from deciding that it looked as if the weather was more settled than it had been and it would probably be fine again tomorrow, barely noticed it.

Her road went downhill again. She passed the bank house where the Frasers lived, and walked on to where the small grey stone church stood in its small glen. There was a hurrying burn just beyond it, it had a backing of trees, and the manse, also built of the same silver grey stone, stood at right angles to it. To it thirty years ago Morag had come as a bride and it had been her home ever since. Neither she nor David had ever had any desire for change.

The minister, busy in one corner of his garden, turned to look at her as she came through the gateway. 'Hello, Morag. Yes, I remembered,' he assured her, his eyes twinkling.

'Good,' his wife said, but absently.

'Come in, David will you. I've something to tell you. Something terrible has happened.'

'What?' David Sinclair dropped his tools and followed his wife through the open front door. 'What is it, Morag?' he was serious. 'Some accident?'

'No, no, nothing like that.' Morag had crossed the minute hall to the big kitchen. She put her basket on the table, automatically looked at the switch on her cooker and then sat down looking dolefully at her husband. The minister was watching her anxiously, waiting for what was to come. 'I can't get the car today after all. Hamish has discovered he needs some part which he can't get for at least two days.'

'The car?' David looked surprised and then he smiled in relief. 'I thought at least there must have been a landslide or a big accident at the forestry camp.' He sat down, facing his wife. 'What's wrong with the car? Can't he fix it at all?' He was not mechanically minded and preferred to leave the driving of their small car to Morag.

'He says not.' She told him what was wrong.

'Well, it's unfortunate,' David said mildly. 'You'll just have to tell Bridget to get the train and the bus right through. It'll be extra tiring for her, but she can go to bed as soon as she gets here.'

'If that were all!' Morag said darkly. 'It's much worse than that. When I was in the store I was telling Mrs Macleod and young Ledoux came in. He said he was going to Inverness tomorrow and he would take me in.'

For a moment her husband stared at her. 'Then that solves it nicely, doesn't it? Kind of him to offer.'

Morag looked at him with exasperation. 'Oh, David, you are obtuse! He's to bring me out again and Bridget will be there too. She'll have to meet him,' she said tragically.

For one moment David looked at her as if he had not heard aright, then he threw back his head and laughed heartily. 'Oh, Morag, Morag!' He wiped his eyes and shook his head at her. 'Don't tell me you've been imagining there could ever be anything between that big fellow, Ledoux and our little Bridget. I can think of nothing more unlikely, impossible!'

Morag smiled reluctantly. 'I know it sounds silly. But strange things happen.'

'But nothing as strange as that!' The minister was still laughing. 'Why, those two must be poles apart. With not a thing in common. I know Bridget is a dear child, but a man like Ledoux will never even see her. As for Bridget she's so shy if she had to say more than two words to him she'd be frightened out of her wits.'

'I know,' Morag said again, complacently this time. 'Bridget could never like a man like that.'

'So what are you worrying about? After all she's bound to meet him some time. He is living here at present. And you know everybody knows everybody in our village.'

'Yes. But that would be just a casual passing of the time of day. Don't you see, David, this — travelling with him all the way from Inverness — makes something particular of it. I suppose I might even have to ask him in for a cup of tea when we do get back.' The disagreeable thought had just occurred to Morag and she grimaced.

'Now, Morag,' her husband said severely, 'that's not like you. The young man is doing us a good turn. Accept it gracefully. After all,' he went on firmly, 'I have never heard anything to his detriment. And neither, I am sure, have you.'

'No,' Mrs Sinclair admitted but doubtfully. 'It is just — Mrs Macleod was saying today that Mrs Robertson says he has all the young women guests fair drooling over him. I would hate people to start talking about Bridget being one of his conquests.'

'Rubbish!' David said. 'Drooling! What a word! Gossip! Is he drooling over them? But what do you expect?

Ledoux is a big, handsome colourful fellow, after all.'

'Handsome?' Morag said doubtfully. 'He's certainly colourful,' she went on tartly. 'You should have seen his shirt today. Hideous! I hope he wears something more sober tomorrow.'

Next morning Mrs Sinclair was ready and waiting before nine o'clock. She was a pretty, graceful woman, who carried her years well. Her hair still kept its golden lights, her complexion was fresh and, minister's wife though she was, she was not above using at least some artificial aides. As the mother of three daughters she had, she declared, to keep up with them. Like her husband she was slight of figure, but though he was of medium height, she was a small woman. She dressed quietly but with taste and she knew that in her village she set a pattern which the other women were very ready to follow. Today she was wearing a small blue hat and had slipped a light coat over her matching blue dress. And now that the

17

die was cast, as it were, she was looking forward to her few hours of shopping in Inverness. Not that she had got rid entirely of her misgivings about her daughter, but she hoped that Bridget, as her father had suggested she would be, would be too shy to say much. And of course there would no question of Bridget sitting other than in the back of the car. As David had told her she was worrying unnecessarily.

The minister had gone into the front garden to see how his dahlias were coming out and promptly at nine o'clock she heard him call. She picked up her basket and went down the path, looking towards the young man getting out of the car with a certain grimness. But at least he had on a jacket today, and he was wearing a collar and tie.

David was greeting him cheerfully. 'It's good of you to come to our rescue today, Mr Ledoux.'

'It's a pleasure. Lucky I had to go in.' He smiled at Morag as she joined them. 'Good morning, Mrs Sinclair.' He took her basket from her and put it into the back of the car and then held the front door for her to get in. Morag returned his greeting and got into the car. 'You don't feel like a trip to Inverness yourself, Mr Sinclair?' the young man asked.

David smiled and shook his head. 'My wife likes to do her shopping on her own.'

Ledoux laughed, shut the door after Morag and went round to get back into the driver's seat. He put a hand up to the minister and Mrs Sinclair called a few words to him.

'He's off to visit a farm about three miles round the point yonder,' she said.

'How will he go? Will he have to walk?'

'No, no, he has his bicycle.' Morag settled back comfortably in her seat. Seated close to him like this her driver looked even bigger and broader than he did at other times. 'We've a fine day for our run, Mr Ledoux,' she said pleasantly.

Ledoux smiled. 'It's a beautiful morning,' he agreed. 'I'm glad for you, Mrs Sinclair. For myself I could have done with a fine day like this at the camp. We've had so much wet weather this last month that I'm not as far advanced as I had hoped to be. I must stop now at the end of the track to speak to my assistant, but I won't keep you waiting long.' They were past the post office and had taken the rising road which led away from the shore of the bay, and about half a mile from the manse, he pulled into a lay-by and stopped the car. 'Just two minutes, Mrs Sinclair,' he said cheerfully and got out.

Morag watched him stride quickly across the road to the end of the track which she knew led into the well-grown forest where the squad were working. A land rover was standing waiting, two men beside it, and Ledoux stood talking to them. He was certainly very dark, but at least he was dressed more soberly than he normally was. Not that that said much, for his trousers were a light fawn and his shirt was green. But his jacket was tweed and a mixture of browns and fawns which even David might have worn. And he was wearing a tie, though it was not one which she would have chosen, though she had to admit that young Dave when he was last at home had had one as brightly patterned. So it must be the fashion. But Dave, of course, was only nineteen and Mr Ledoux must be — in his late twenties or thirty David had thought.

But he was coming back. 'All set now,' he said as he started his engine. 'We'll probably be in just before eleven. That satisfactory for you, Mrs Sinclair?'

'Fine for me,' Morag agreed. 'You have a comfortable car, Mr Ledoux. Bigger than ours, so you'll get more speed out of it.'

'It's not a road for much speed though,' the young man smiled and pulled his car into a passing place to allow another vehicle coming towards them to go past on the single track road.

Morag studied his profile as he started off again. Seated on his left hand she could see distinctly the scar down his left cheek. She wondered how he had got it, but she could hardly ask him. In some drunken brawl perhaps she thought, and then felt ashamed of herself. For she had never seen Ledoux drunk, or heard of him having been so. Or brawling either for that matter. It was just, she told herself complacently, that her instinct told her to distrust anyone who seemed to be, as Ledoux was, larger than life.

Ledoux, conscious of her scrutiny, gave her a quick look. 'I believe your little girl has been ill, Mrs Sinclair.'

'Yes,' Morag answered and hesitated. Had he, somehow, got hold of a wrong impression about Bridget? 'She got herself a rare dose of cold through getting a real wetting. That was in June when it was more like winter than summer. They thought it was flu but it turned to pneumonia and she was whisked off to hospital. Poor Bridget!'

There was genuine feeling in Mrs Sinclair's voice, and for the moment she had forgotten her reservations about the man to whom she talked. 'Yes, she's had a bad time. A whole month in hospital and a hard fight for it.'

'Poor kid,' Ledoux said sympathetically. 'Do I take it she has been in hospital in Edinburgh? That must have been very worrying for you having her so far away. And lonely for her too.'

'Her aunt lives in Edinburgh — she had been staying with her. The minister and I did go down to see her at the beginning, and one of her married sisters lives in Glasgow, so she has been through to see her.'

'I hope she is much better now.'

'Oh, she's fine, she says. The doctors say she's all right but she's to have two months at home in Achinlaig to build her up again.'

'You'll be glad to have her home,' Ledoux again pulled into a passing place, waiting for a couple of cars to pass them. 'Have you heard from your son, Mrs Sinclair? Isn't it Norway he's gone to?'

'Yes.' Morag laughed. 'Chopping bits of rock to find minerals he says. We'd a card from him,' she said dryly. 'That's all we'll ever get from Dave.'

After that they did not talk much. Mrs Sinclair produced one or two village anecdotes and the young man commented on the fine scenery, the loveliness of Loch Maree alongside which their road was taking them, the magnificence of the mountains. Morag looked at him curiously and agreed that it was pretty. For her scenery was merely a background to living and nothing more.

They arrived in Inverness by eleven o'clock and after confirming that he would be at the station to pick up both her and her daughter at the time the train was due in, Ledoux dropped Mrs Sinclair off and went. For the rest of the morning Morag enjoyed her shopping and then went to a café to have a light lunch. She was in the station, getting herself a ticket to take her on to the platform, in good time to meet the Edinburgh train. She hoped that Bridget was not too tired after her journey, for she had only come out of hospital last Thursday. But she had sounded very cheerful when she had spoken to her on the phone on Sunday and declared that she was very fit. Frances, too, had said she was sure the journey would not be too much for her. Well, once she got her home she meant to keep her there. She could do with her help in the house, and if the bank would let her take a part-time job with Mr Fraser in Achinlaig instead of working full-time in Edinburgh, that would be ideal.

She looked about her to see if there were any porters near, but there was not one in sight. And — the train was signalled. For once it was going to be on time. A few minutes later it pulled in slowly and Mrs Sinclair walked up the platform, looking for a sight of Bridget's fair head at a window. She saw her and went forward as the train stopped. A man got down from the carriage and behind him Bridget was smiling and putting a hand up to her mother. She got down nimbly, turning to lift her hold-all and her suitcase down on to the platform.

Morag Sinclair, looking critically at her daughter, thought with an unexpected dismay, that she looked as if a puff of wind would blow her over. For Bridget, always slender, looked even thinner and smaller, her fair skin had a transparent look. But there was a brightness in her dark blue eyes and her fair hair, with its golden lights, had a sheen about it. When last she had been home Bridget's hair had fallen to her shoulders, but it had been cut in hospital and now it curled prettily about her head.

She was smiling warmly now, as she bent to kiss her mother. 'Hello, mother. How are you?' She glanced at her mother's well-filled basket. 'Have you had that good morning's shopping?'

'Aye, I have that.' Morag patted her daughter's shoulder. 'How are you feeling now, Bridget? No ill-effects from the long journey?'

'I'm fine,' Bridget said stoutly. 'A bit dusty, that's all.'

'Well, you're looking very nice in your new suit, Bridget!' Mrs Sinclair gave an approving nod at her daughter's choice. Bridget's cardigan suit was a deep, soft blue and was edged with braid of a lighter shade. 'Does it still fit you?' she asked dryly.

Bridget laughed. 'I'd to put a bit of a tuck in the skirt, but no doubt in a week or so I'll have to let it out again.' She looked about her. 'I suppose there isn't a porter in sight?'

'I haven't seen one. Maybe if I take your holdall?'

'It's all right, Mother. I'll manage. You've got your basket.' She moved the straps of her handbag up her arm and picked up the holdall in one hand and the suitcase in the other. 'Lead on,

Mother. How far away is the car?'

'I haven't got the car, Bridget. Oh, it was so vexing! It broke down when your father was coming home in it on Sunday night, and Hamish has to send away for something or other.' She glanced at her daughter, coming slowly at her side. 'Maybe I should give you a hand with those, Bridget?'

'It's all right, Mother,' Bridget said again. 'Did Aunt Janet bring you in? But I thought they were going away.'

'Oh, yes, they're away. Mr Ledoux brought me in, and is taking us out.'

'Ledoux? Do I know him?' Bridget asked but without much interest. She was breathing heavily for her case was heavy and she was glad they were nearing the barrier.

'No, no,' Morag said hastily. 'He's one of the Forestry men. He heard I needed a lift and offered as he was coming in to Inverness today.'

'Kind of him,' Bridget said and put her suitcase down. They had reached the barrier. 'You go on, Mother. I'll catch you when I find my ticket.' She put her hand into her jacket pocket, and her mother went on through the barrier.

Ledoux stepped forward and took Morag's basket from her. 'I'll take that, Mrs Sinclair.' He looked beyond her. 'Has your daughter not come on the train?'

'Yes. That's Bridget coming now.'

Ledoux's stare of surprise was momentary. He took a step past the ticket collector and put a hand on the girl's suitcase. 'Let me take that,' he said quietly and as Bridget looked up at him saw a girl whose dark blue eyes seemed enormous in her pale face. His thoughts were much as her mother's had been. As he lifted the heavy case he felt as if he should be carrying Bridget as well as her suitcase to the car. He stepped back and Bridget gave her ticket to the collector and followed him.

'This is my daughter Bridget, Mr Ledoux,' Mrs Sinclair said as they halted beside her. 'Mr Ledoux is kindly giving us a lift back to Achinlaig, Bridget.'

Bridget smiled at the man. He was a big man, she thought and he was very dark. She held out her hand, then realizing that he had his hands fully occupied with her suitcase and her mother's basket, dropped it.

But Ledoux had put down the case and his big hand closed about Bridget's clasping it gently but firmly for a moment. 'Pleased to meet you, Bridget,' he said. He gave her mother a quick grin. 'Mrs Sinclair, I had it all wrong, hadn't I? I was expecting a schoolgirl.'

'Were you?' Morag smiled, but warily. She had already decided that he had the wrong idea, and she thought it was a pity that he had not been able to keep it.

'I suppose I just took it for granted that she was your youngest and came after Dave.' He put his hand out and took Bridget's holdall from her and then the coat she had over her arm. 'I'll take those too, Bridget,' he said.

'Oh, I can carry something,' Bridget protested.

'No,' the young man said and picked up the suitcase again. 'The car is in the square, Mrs Sinclair.' He led the way to the station entrance.

Behind him Bridget whispered to her mother as they followed. 'What did you say his name was?'

'Ledoux,' Morag answered cautiously. 'He's Canadian. French-Canadian, your father says,' she added and grimaced.

'Well, he seems kind,' Bridget said quietly. 'I'm glad I haven't to carry that case any further.'

In the station square Ledoux was putting the case and the bags into the boot of his car. As they came up to him he shut it firmly and opened both front and back doors. 'Are you finished your shopping, Mrs Sinclair? Or — ' he looked at the girl, 'does Bridget want to go and have something to eat or drink before we set off?'

'I'm all finished, thank you, Mr Ledoux,' Morag said sedately. 'Your aunt would give you some sandwiches, Bridget, I suppose?'

'Yes, Mother,' Bridget answered. 'And there was a buffet car on the train, so I went along and had some coffee.'

'Did you?' Her mother looked surprised. To her Bridget was still the shy girl who would never do anything on her own initiative. 'Have you finished your business, Mr Ledoux?'

'Yes. All set, Mrs Sinclair. Where are you going to sit.' He looked from one to the other, expecting that Mrs Sinclair would want to sit in the back with her daughter.

But Morag had no such idea. Used to taking the centre of the stage in her own small world, she disliked sitting in the back of a car. 'Oh, I'll come in front with you,' she said. 'Bridget, if you sit to the right you'll not be bothered with the sun.' Bridget got in obediently. 'I think I'll take my coat off,' Morag went on. 'It's going to be hot.'

'Yes, it is hot now,' Ledoux took Mrs Sinclair's coat from her, took off his own jacket and laid them on the seat next to Bridget. 'What about you, Bridget?' he asked.

Bridget shook her head. 'Later perhaps,' she said and smiled. She wondered what his christian name was. Her mother said Mr Ledoux but then that was her mother's way with anyone who was not part of her own tightly-knit community. But maybe he had not been long in Achinlaig.

Mrs Sinclair turned to look at her as Ledoux went round and got behind the wheel. 'Have you had a card from Dave, Bridget?'

'I'd a letter,' Bridget answered. 'He seems to be enjoying himself.'

'A letter!' her mother said dryly. 'My, you were favoured. Your father and I had to do with a card between us. Janet and Alan got themselves away last Thursday,' she went on and then sat forward as Ledoux started his car. 'That's Doctor and Mrs Murray,' she told him. 'They're away off to Paris.'

'Yes. The doctor told me,' Ledoux

took his car into the line of traffic.

Behind them Bridget leaned back in her seat gratefully. She knew she had not yet got back her usual energy, and carrying her case for even those few yards had taken it out of her. It was as well Mr Ledoux had appeared when he did. She looked at him, but seated directly behind him as she was she could see no more of him than his wide shoulders in his green shirt, and his thick black hair.

Her mother turned to ask her an occasional question, and Bridget answered, but for the most part Mrs Sinclair sat looking forward. As far as the girl could hear the conversation in the front was desultory. For herself she was glad to sit quietly looking about her as they left the busy streets of Inverness and took the northward road which skirted the Beauly Firth.

She was a quiet girl, Bridget Sinclair, and had always been known in Achinlaig as the gentle one of the minister's three daughters. But if she was quiet and gentle Bridget also had character. She had her mother's colouring, but for the rest she was herself and not like anyone else in her family. She had a firm and resolute chin, and her dark blue eyes and her generous mouth reflected the warmth of her nature. She had spirit, too, and was quite determined to get back her strength, and was the last person to try to hide behind any real or fancied weakness.

Mr Ledoux's car had a good turn of speed, it was more powerful than her father's or that of her uncle, but he did not drive too fast or recklessly. If he had, she thought with an amused twinkle, her mother would have been telling him so. But presently they left the main north road and took the narrow single track road which would lead them to the west coast. Now she decided he was a considerate driver, for he pulled into the passing places and did not go on boldly expecting the oncoming vehicle to do so.

Just before their road for Loch Maree

branched away from that which led north and west to Ullapool, there was a filling station at the left of the road, and Ledoux pulled in and stopped. He told Mrs Sinclair that he wanted his tank filled up and got out as the attendant came forward. From her corner Bridget looked at him. He was certainly a very tall man, he had very broad shoulders, but he was not flabby with it. His face, now that she could see it, was thin if anything, there were deep lines at the sides of his big mouth, he had a strong jaw and chin.

'If it stays fine like this you'll be able to sit out in the garden, Bridget,' her mother turned to speak to her.

'Yes. A few days of sunshine and fresh air and I'll be ready for anything,' Bridget said cheerfully and smiled at Morag.

She looked out of her window again and saw that Ledoux had turned and was looking at her. He smiled and she smiled back. She watched him pay the attendant and then step back to the car.

He leaned in, looking back at her.

'Are you all right, Bridget? Quite comfortable?' he asked.

'Oh, she's fine,' Mrs Sinclair said.

Bridget answered for herself. 'I'm very comfortable, thank you,' she said. 'And I'm enjoying the drive very much,' she said warmly.

'The best is yet to come, as you'll know,' Ledoux said. 'Well, sing out if we come to a bad bit of road and I'm going too fast.'

'Thank you,' Bridget said again. He had a scar down his left cheek and she wondered how he had got it, but her thoughts did not go in the same direction as her mother's had done.

Ledoux got into the car and they moved away again. Bridget slipped off her jacket and leaned back again. She was glad that Mr Ledoux had made his generous offer to her mother to bring them all this way. It was much nicer travelling like this than having to take the train with all its many stops, and then having to get herself and her luggage from train to bus. She looked about her at the changing colours of the moors, the purple carpet which was spread over them now that August was here. She looked with pleasure at the beautiful loch stretching away in its magnificent setting, admired the colours of trees and mountains and water as the twisting road took them over the country she had known and loved all her life, and so to the sea.

In a minute Ledoux had slowed, was looking behind him, then taking his car across the road to stop in front of the manse. The minister was in the garden, and he came forward, opening the rear door and greeting his daughter. Ledoux got out too and went round to open the other door for Mrs Sinclair to get out and then going to take the luggage from his boot.

'Well, you've had a splendid day for your trip,' the minister said cheerfully. 'Enjoyed it, Morag?' He exchanged an expressive look with his wife as she came round the car.

'Very nice,' Morag said. She smiled at the young man. 'I'm sure we're very grateful to you, Mr Ledoux. Now I'll be making some tea in a few minutes,' she went on pleasantly, 'so will you come in and have some with us?'

Ledoux smiled. 'Thank you, Mrs Sinclair,' he said, 'but if you'll excuse me I won't. I want to get out to the camp now. I want to catch the men before they go off.' He looked at the minister. 'They never work late on a Tuesday, and I want to arrange for them to do overtime for the rest of the week. Catch this fine weather.'

'Yes,' David Sinclair smiled. 'But I've the tea all ready and the kettle on the boil, so — in two minutes?'

Ledoux hesitated and glanced at Bridget. She was standing quietly to one side, looking at them. But though those big eyes of hers were dark and shining, there were shadows under them, and there was no colour in her cheeks. She would be tired and besides, she would want to be alone with her family. He shook his head. 'Thank you,' he said again, 'but I'll just get straight on if you don't mind. I'll put these inside for you.' He picked up the luggage and carried everything up the path before the minister could even offer to help.

Mrs Sinclair followed him up. That had passed off quite well, and David could not say she had been inhospitable. Though there had been no need for him to press the young man. No doubt Ledoux knew he could not be at ease with them. And David had been right about Bridget. She would never have anything to say to a man like he was.

'Thank you,' she said again graciously as Ledoux put down the suitcase and the other bags. He put up a hand and went back down the path.

At the gateway, Bridget was still standing, admiring her father's garden, of which she knew he was very proud. She looked up at Ledoux as he came abreast of her, smiling at him warmly.

'Thank you very much, Mr Ledoux. I've enjoyed the drive home very much.'

'A pleasure — ' there was a sudden gleam in Ledoux's dark eyes as he hesitated, 'Bridget.'

There was a slight flush of pink in Bridget's cheeks as she watched him get back into his car, swing it round and go back the way they had come. He was not so very much older than she was and he seemed nice. He called her Bridget as, of course, everyone in Achinlaig did, but she could hardly use his christian name too when she did not even know it. She followed her father up the path and into the house.

2

It was not until they were having their supper that night that Ledoux was even mentioned in the manse. While they had their tea Bridget had to tell her parents what she had done during the few days since she had come out of hospital, give her mother news about Morag's sister, with whom the girl had lived while working in Edinburgh, tell them of when her sister, Sheena, had visited her from Glasgow. Mrs Sinclair had all the small news of the village to relate, but somehow the name of the Canadian did not come in at all.

Afterwards Bridget had gone to her own room to unpack, settling in to the familiar surroundings for the two months she was to stay at home, and which would be the longest time she had spent at Achinlaig for over four years now. When she came down again supper was ready. As the minister had no calls to take him out that night they were having it early, Morag said, so that Bridget could get away to bed early.

'Yes,' Bridget smiled and agreed. 'I'm sure I'll sleep very quickly tonight. It must be the air.'

'That's what you need, Bridget,' David Sinclair smiled gently at his daughter. 'Plenty of good air and a few platefuls of your mother's porridge.'

Bridget laughed. 'I'll be fine in a day or two,' she said stoutly. 'Though I must say,' she admitted, 'I was very glad when Mr Ledoux appeared to carry my suitcase this afternoon.'

She was looking at her father and missed the tightening of her mother's lips.

'There wasn't a porter in sight,' Morag said briskly. 'Did you manage to get one in Edinburgh, Bridget?'

'Yes,' Bridget answered, but there was something she wanted to know and she was not to be side-tracked. 'Did you say he had something to do with the forestry, mother?'

'Who? Oh, Ledoux. Yes.' Mrs Sinclair picked up a plate to hold it out to her daughter.

Her husband gave her a look of amusement. 'He's got a squad of men working in that well-grown forest about half a mile or so out on the Loch Maree road,' he told Bridget. 'He's over from Canada doing a spell over here. MacNeil says he's an expert in his particular field and they're very glad to have him.'

Bridget took a drink of her tea. 'He seems a quiet man,' she said simply.

Her mother stared at her. 'Quiet! Ledoux?'

The minister chuckled, but he looked curiously at his daughter. Had she, perhaps, a perception which his wife lacked?

Bridget was surprised. 'Don't you think so, mother?'

'I do not,' Morag was emphatic. 'He is extremely loud.'

'I don't think Bridget means it quite

in the way you do, Morag,' David put in. He smiled at Bridget. 'Your mother has an aversion to the shirts the young man wears.'

'Shirts!' Bridget laughed. 'Quite sober today surely?'

'Green! I'd hardly say sober,' Morag said dryly. 'But wait till you see him on an ordinary day. Absolutely hideous!' She remembered something. 'If you see him. As a matter of fact,' she went on carefully, 'I was afraid the very sight of him today would frighten you, Bridget.'

Bridget looked at her mother in astonishment. Why she should be frightened of Mr Ledoux, who had been both kind and courteous to her she could not think. 'Why ever should it, Mother?' she asked.

'Well, look at him!' Morag said tartly. 'So huge, so black, so flamboyant. So loud! For myself,' she went on complacently, 'I never could abide a man as big and dark as that, could you?' She invited her daughter to agree with her and then shivered delicately. 'I would hate to be touched by a man like that, wouldn't you?'

There was a faint colour in Bridget's cheeks, but she did not answer. David Sinclair was laughing and shaking his head at his wife.

'Morag. Morag! I'm thinking it's as well for me you didn't fancy a big, dark man.'

Morag gave him a reluctant grin. 'I suppose somebody must fancy that type,' she went on disdainfully. 'He's certainly playing havoc among the women visitors at the hotel.'

Bridget looked down at her plate and missed her father's frown. 'Now, Morag,' he said severely, 'that's gossip. As far as we know the young man is doing a good job, and today he did us a good turn. After all he is a young, single man, and as he's living in the hotel he can hardly avoid being friendly with the people staying there. And why shouldn't he, if he wants to?'

'Why, indeed!' Morag said tartly, and put a great deal of meaning into the two words. But she changed the subject and presently Bridget, having helped her mother to clear the table and wash up the dishes, said goodnight and went off to her own room. She paused a moment in front of her mirror, looking at herself critically. She grimaced and gave a small sigh. She walked over to her window and stood a moment. The early August night was still light and there was not a sound. Her room did not look to the front, so she could see no more than a rising hillside, a group of trees. But the air was fresh and lovely. She turned slowly and began to undress. She was very tired, she had to admit.

The next two days were fine and really hot and Bridget was content to spend most of her time relaxing in the small garden behind the house. In the mornings she helped her mother by making beds and washing dishes, cleaning potatoes and doing some dusting. But after that she took a book and went out to enjoy the fresh warm air. Not that she read at all. Instead she leaned back and let the sunshine on her skin lull her to sleep. She was being lazy she told herself, but the doctor at the hospital had told her not to force herself, she had to go easy, her strength would come back.

The minister, coming back from an afternoon visit, and finding her sound asleep, looked at her for a long anxious moment and went into the house to find his wife.

'Bridget is asleep,' he said. 'I'm wishing Alan Murray was back, so that he can have a look at her.'

'Aye,' Morag agreed. 'But they said she needed building up. Frances told me what the doctor at the hospital said. She's all right. And she's only been out of hospital for a week.'

'I suppose we'll just need to be patient. She seems to be eating all right.'

'She is that. And, mind you, I did think she had a bit more colour in her cheeks today.'

On the Friday morning when Bridget came down for her breakfast her mother, looking at her critically, decided that she did have colour which she had not had on Tuesday, the shadows under her eyes had gone. Of course she was still much too thin, her skin too transparent, but she was improving. Bridget, she thought complacently, had always been a home girl, and now she was back at home she would soon recover her strength and settle down to the life her mother was planning for her.

So that when Bridget suggested she should walk to the store and do the shopping, Morag made no demur. She was not to get her car back till that afternoon, and had no desire to walk the mile to the store and the mile back herself.

Swinging her basket Bridget set off up the undulating road. She felt much more energetic this morning, and it was a lovely day. She might even meet someone she knew. Not that there would be many people in the village to meet at this time of morning. But to go on sitting in their secluded garden, pleasant as it had been, she would never see anybody.

She looked out over the blue waters of the bay to the distant islands, seeing it all in a way her mother never did. Bridget loved Achinlaig, the glorious sweep of sea and lochs, of mountains and forests surrounding it. She hoped that someday she would be able to live in the country. Not at Achinlaig of course. Much as she loved it she did not want to spend all her life here even if she could. But she preferred country to town. But — she smiled at her thoughts — in certain circumstances she might even see a town as the one place she wanted to be.

She walked on, past the garage and the hotel, and down the long hill to the store. A few cars travelling northward passed her, but she met no one she knew, and there was only Mrs Macleod at the store to greet her cheerfully, to ask her how she was, to say she was pleased to see her back home. Bridget lingered a few minutes talking to her, and then set off home again. Outside the bank house she paused. Yesterday her mother had said she had seen Mary Fraser and she was going to come and see Bridget. But there was no sign of Mary in the gardens or near the windows, and as the bank opened on a Friday morning, her husband would be busy.

Bridget went on, but as she walked into the manse she heard Mrs Fraser's voice. She opened the living room door, smiling cheerfully. 'Hello, Mary. I was looking for you as I passed your house.'

'Hello, Bridget!' Mary Fraser looked the girl over critically. She was a cheerful woman in her forties, who was always ready to play second-in-command to Mrs Sinclair when there was anything to arrange in the village. With no family of her own she always had time to serve on any committee, to do the hard work in arranging this or

51

that. 'My, you won't need to slim, will you, Bridget,' she said now candidly. 'But you're looking bonny, and much better than I feared you'd be from what Morag was saying yesterday to — '

'Her walk has given her a nice colour,' Mrs Sinclair, busy pouring coffee, put in so that Bridget lost the name of whoever it was to whom her mother had been talking. 'I've just made coffee. Go and get yourself a cup, and come and have some, Bridget.'

Bridget went off, putting her basket in the kitchen and coming back with another cup. 'I'm glad I didn't miss you, Mary,' she said as her mother poured coffee into the cup for her.

'Oh, I'd have waited. I want to see you about something. Thank you, Morag.' She accepted a shortbread finger and bit into it. 'Did you bring these from Inverness? It was lucky Ledoux was going in on Tuesday. He seems to run a nice car. Did you enjoy the drive out, Bridget?'

Bridget smiled warmly. 'Very much.'

'What were you saying about Alec, Mary?' Morag asked.

'Oh yes.' Mary was side-tracked from that dangerous subject. 'He's going off down to Perth this afternoon. Some bankers' conference or other, and there's this dance in the village hall on Saturday night — the August holiday dance, you'll remember, Morag — and as I'm the organizer I've got to be there to keep an eye on things. And Alec won't be here to take me and bring me home. So I thought I'd persuade Bridget to come with me. How about it, Bridget? Then we can walk each other home, as we've all done on other occasions.'

'Why, yes, I'd like to come.' Bridget brightened. Everybody attended the village dances. 'Saturday, you say, I'd forgotten it was the August holiday.'

'Oh, I don't know, Bridget,' Mrs Sinclair said doubtfully. 'Not yet. I don't think she's fit for that yet, Mary.'

'It'll do her good,' Mary said

cheerfully. 'She doesn't need to dance all night.'

'It'll be fun to watch,' Bridget said. 'I'll restrict myself to a few dances.' Her eyes twinkled. 'If I'm asked!'

Morag's look was still doubtful. 'I don't want you to tire yourself, Bridget. Not till you get your strength back properly.' That Bridget should even want to go when she had a perfect excuse not to do so was unexpected, for usually she liked to keep in the background, was shy at mixing with people, even those she had known all her life.

'I'll not tire myself,' Bridget promised. 'I suppose you're going to have the usual mixture — old and new, Mary?'

'Yes. And this will be the last dance till the middle or the end of September. Everybody will be anxious to see Bridget, Morag,' she went on. 'I'd have suggested you came too, but I know you don't like doing anything on a Saturday night.'

'No,' Mrs Sinclair agreed. Should she

go just to keep an eye on Bridget, see that she did not do too much. But Mary would do that. 'David always likes a quiet night on a Saturday before the morning service and I've always stayed with him. Well, you'll have to see she takes it quietly, Mary.'

Bridget laughed. 'Mother thinks I'm still seventeen,' she said lightly. 'Well, I'll restrict myself to say, four dances, and for the rest of the time I'll watch everybody enjoying themselves.'

'I'm sure after a month on a hospital bed, you deserve a bit of fun,' Mary said stoutly. 'Don't you agree, Morag?'

'Of course.' Morag smiled. Just sitting in the background watching others dancing would be enjoyment for Bridget. And, of course, her family had always been expected to join in anything going on in the village. There was no Big House in the district and the minister and his family had always occupied the place that any such family would have had. Morag had always accepted and enjoyed that role and, privately, thought she played it well. And, as she intended Bridget to stay at home after this she would have to learn to be her mother's understudy when the occasion arose. As for her having to meet Ledoux again on Saturday that would have to happen some time. As David had said she had been foolish in her worries in that direction. Bridget after all, was too much like herself to even think of a man like he was. And Ledoux, even if he had stopped his car while she was talking to Mary yesterday to ask if Bridget was all right after her journey, would have plenty to amuse him at the dance. No doubt he would speak to her politely as was due to the minister's daughter but that would be all. 'I expect you'll be getting some of the people from the hotel, Mary.'

'Oh, yes, I expect so. I think we'll get enough to make it pay on Saturday. If you call for me about eight, Bridget, that will do. It's starting at seven-thirty, but I don't need to be there at the beginning.'

'Right, Mary,' Bridget agreed. 'I'll be there. We'll finish about eleven-thirty I suppose?' She smiled. 'I'm looking forward to it. I'll need to decide what I'm going to wear.'

For the rest of the day and for a good part of Saturday she gave a great deal of thought to which dress she should wear. Not that the village dances required elaborate toilettes nor that she had an extensive wardrobe, but she wanted to look her best. And pale and uninteresting as she was now some of the colours she normally wore did nothing for her. After all, she did not want her village friends to think she was still ill, to have them condoling with her when she was there to enjoy herself. She tried on a blue dress which usually suited her well, but it made her look completely colourless. A green did nothing for her. She looked doubtfully at a coral pink which she had bought in the spring and only worn once before her illness. Probably it too would take away all her colour. She slipped it over her head and maybe because she was flushed with her exertions or its colour reflected in her cheeks, decided it would do. Self-coloured in a rayon which looked like silk, it was sleeveless and it had a wide belt, which she had to tighten well in. With it she would wear the gold brooch which had been her family's joint twenty-first birthday gift to her.

When she came downstairs next evening ready to go to the bank house for Mary, her mother looked at her and smiled. Bridget was turning into a pretty child but, of course, there was nothing flamboyant about her. She told her to enjoy herself, but to remember not to be too energetic or dance too much. Bridget laughed and promised and went off.

It had been a very hot day and the evening air was still warm as she walked the short way up the hill to the Frasers' house. Mary let her in, admired her dress, and went off upstairs to finish her own dressing.

'How are you feeling, Bridget? All right?' she asked when she came down again a few minutes later.

'Of course,' Bridget said cheerfully. 'I'm not an invalid now.'

'Well, I'll need to see you don't tire yourself or I don't know what Morag will say to me.' She glanced at her watch. 'Right. I expect most of them will be there by now,' she went on as they went down the path and turned up the road. 'When it's an early stop they get started quicker.'

'I suppose I'll know most people there,' Bridget said carefully.

'Oh, yes,' Mary said cheerfully. 'There'll be a party from the hotel, but they usually keep to themselves. Then there's the Forestry men. The younger ones always come. And Mr Ledoux. You've met him. He's a striking looking man, isn't he?' Mary went on casually. If she had been canvassed her opinion would have been much the same as David Sinclair's.

'He comes, does he?'

'Oh, yes. When he first arrived I told him he had to come. He's useful if there's too much exuberance among the young ones. I hope Kate Macleod managed to get those sausage rolls from the baker this morning,' she added worriedly. 'I meant to check with her and I forgot.'

Bridget smiled as she listened to Mary hoping that this one had done something or that one had remembered to take something. But she was a good organizer and took her duties seriously. And it was a beautiful night. There was a faint pink behind the islands, it was still very warm. It would be fine for their walk home at midnight.

They went past the hotel and down the hill to where the village hall sat back from the road not far from the store. It was a low building of stone, with a wooden platform around it, reached by a few steps, and as they neared they could hear the sound of the music coming out of the open doorway. They put their coats in the tiny cloakroom and Bridget followed Mary into the crowded hall.

Now that she was here her natural shyness made her stay close behind Mary, but she did give a quick look down the long room. Yes, Mr Ledoux was there. She recognized him from his tall figure and the back of his head, for he had his back to her and was about half way down the hall, partnering a tall girl in a dress gaily patterned in reds and golds. Someone from the hotel, she decided. Mary had said they usually kept to themselves, but perhaps Mr Ledoux, if he discovered she was here would come to speak to her. She would like to talk to him, to look at him, to decide if she had been right in her first impression of him, or if it was her mother who was right. She turned to speak to the group of older people who crowded round Mary, who wanted to know how Bridget was, and did not see Ledoux swing round suddenly and look at her.

Guiding his partner down the room

he had smiled at Effie Cameron dancing past with her husband and then heard Effie exclaim, 'Why there's young Bridget! I did hear she was home. My, she does look — '

But however Effie thought Bridget was looking was lost, as they passed on. Ledoux turned quickly, looking towards the doorway. Yes, it was Bridget. She seemed to have come with Mrs Fraser who had apparently just arrived. Bridget still looked as fragile as a windflower, but there was a pretty colour in her cheeks and she was smiling that warm and lovely smile of hers which he had noticed particularly on Tuesday as she talked now to Mrs Macleod from the store and Mrs Laurie whose husband he believed had something to do with the fishing.

He smiled slightly and then realized that his partner was looking at him quizzically. Moira Robinson was not used to her dancing partners being distrait, and she looked at him archly, 'Something amusing?' she questioned.

'Sorry,' Ledoux apologized automatically. 'No. A friend whom I didn't expect to come, has just arrived.' But the music was ceasing and expertly he guided her to where a young man was standing leaning against the wall. 'Your brother doesn't seem to have found a partner yet.' He smiled at the young man as they reached him, gave Moira a little bow, said a formal 'Thank you. If you'll excuse me?' and moved away, threading a way swiftly through the couples returning from the floor.

There was a flash of annoyance in the girl's eyes as her brother laughed. 'That was quick, Moira! No conquest?'

'Oh, he'll be back,' Moira tossed her long black hair. 'He did give me the first dance.'

'He could hardly help himself,' her brother said candidly. 'You fairly fell into his arms.'

Moira flashed him a look of scorn. She looked towards the entrance to which Ledoux was rapidly making his way. There was no one there who would rival her in any way. He would be back.

By now Mary Fraser was making anxious enquiries about her sausage rolls and Bridget's eyes were twinkling as she heard the reassuring news that they were all there as ordered.

'Hello, Bridget,' said a man's voice at her side, and she turned quickly to look up at the big man smiling down at her. 'I didn't think we were to have the pleasure of seeing you here tonight. How are you now? Feeling rested?'

'Oh, yes, thank you. I feel fine,' Bridget said stoutly and smiled warmly.

Mary turned too. 'Hello, Mr Ledoux. I saw you were here.' She smiled at Bridget. 'I think she looks better even from when I saw her yesterday. As Alec had to go off to a conference I persuaded Bridget to come and keep me company. Besides I thought a little liveliness would do her good.'

'I'm sure it will, Mrs Fraser,' Ledoux agreed.

'Mind you,' Mary went on, 'I've promised her mother to see she doesn't do too much. She's not to tire herself.'

'We'll see she doesn't do that,' the man said quietly. 'Are you allowed to dance, Bridget?'

'Yes,' Bridget answered. 'Just a few dances. I know my limitations! Mostly I'm going to watch.'

'Four dances was what you said, Bridget,' Mary said playfully. 'I'll be keeping check.'

'Four.' Ledoux smiled. 'I'll keep check for you, Mrs Fraser. So — may I, Bridget?' He held his hand out to her. 'The next one is just about to start, I think.'

'Thank you,' Bridget said shyly and put her hand in his. Already she was getting much more than she had hoped. Just to be noticed for a few minutes was all she had expected. And — she had been right — he was a quiet man. She glanced at him as she went with him a few yards onto the dance floor. Tonight, he was wearing a dark grey suit and a plain white shirt with a tie which even her mother could not have said was gaudy.

Ledoux caught her look and smiled, keeping her close to him as someone brushed past them. 'We'll wait to see what sort of dance it is to be,' he told her. 'If it's too strenuous we'll sit it out and try the next one.'

But when the music started it was not the wild beat of a modern number and Ledoux put his arm round her gently and guided her forward.

Behind them Mary Fraser watched and then turned away. 'That was nice of him,' she said to Mrs Laurie. 'You'll know he brought Bridget and her mother back from Inverness on Tuesday when the Sinclairs' car had broken down. So — that'll get Bridget into the swim. She's a nice child, but she's always been too self-effacing.'

'Overshadowed by her sisters,' Mrs Laurie said shrewdly. She chuckled. 'I hope she's making out all right now for you could hardly say she and Ledoux were of a size.'

3

But Bridget though her head came no higher than her partner's shoulder had no qualms. Ledoux's arm which had gone round her so gently that she had felt, with a little wry amusement, as if she was something which might break at a touch, was holding her firmly and securely now, his big hand was clasping hers closely. He was suiting his steps to hers, guiding her carefully, and Bridget, relaxing to the rhythm of the music, smiled up at him.

'The little band is playing much better than I remembered it did,' she murmured.

Ledoux, looking down at her, was thinking that Bridget's eyes were as dark and big and shining as he had known they were on Tuesday. His arm tightened slightly as he steered her away from a clumsy couple. 'How long since you were at home in Achinlaig, Bridget?' he asked.

'Easter,' Bridget told him, but they did not talk much. The music died away and Ledoux gave her a little bow and said Thank you. But he kept his arm round her waist and guided her to the side of the room, where chairs and forms were set out against the wall.

'We'll sit this next one out,' he told her. He glanced about him. 'I suppose you know most people here so — ' he smiled, 'before the rest of those four dances get booked, keep one more for me, will you.'

'Yes,' Bridget said shyly and sat down. Now he would leave her, go back to his own party. She saw the girl in the bright dress, with whom he had been dancing when she had arrived looking at them from the other end of the room. But Ledoux had given no glance in that direction. He sat down beside Bridget and looked at her seriously for a moment.

'You do look better, Bridget,' he said

then. 'From what your mother said on Thursday — '

'On Thursday?' Bridget questioned. Her mother had not mentioned seeing Mr Ledoux when she was out on Thursday.

The young man nodded. 'She was talking to Mrs Fraser. I'd been back to the hotel to collect the mail — I do that if I'm expecting anything in particular — so I stopped.' He smiled. 'I wanted to know if you were all right after your journey on Tuesday. From what she said I thought there was no hope of seeing you here tonight.'

Bridget smiled warmly. So he had stopped his car just to enquire for her. Her mother must have forgotten to tell her. 'I was very lazy on Wednesday and Thursday,' she confessed. 'I spent most of the time resting in the garden. But by yesterday morning I was feeling much more energetic. I walked down to the store and back. And when Mary came and asked if I'd come with her tonight I wanted to come.'

'I'm glad,' Ledoux said simply. 'How did you and Mrs Fraser get here, Bridget? Who brought you?'

'We walked. The two of us. That's partly why I came tonight. To keep Mary company. For the walk home too.'

'Mrs Fraser should have given me a ring and I'd have come over for you both,' Ledoux said. 'As for walking home — ' his brows came down. 'Are the two of you thinking of walking that lonely road at that hour? And what about you? For the manse is quite a bit beyond the bank.'

Bridget laughed. 'Oh, there won't be anyone about at that time. And we have a system. Mary comes half way down with me and then walks back as I go forward. So we don't have very far on our own.' Her eyes twinkled as she saw Ledoux's expression.

He shook his head in disbelief. 'Well, you won't be using that system tonight,' he said firmly. 'I'll take you both home. I've the car with me.'

Bridget coloured a little, remembering, hoping he did not think she had been asking for that. 'That's very kind of you,' she said, 'but — ' she hesitated, glancing down the room. Did he not have someone with him? She had thought — but before she could find the right words to say to him Effie Cameron came up to them.

'Hello there, Bridget. Glad to see you back home. How are you now?'

'Very much better now, thank you, Effie,' Bridget smiled. Ledoux had stood up, but again did not move away.

'Good,' Effie said heartily. 'You've had a bad time, haven't you. But I'm glad you could make it here tonight.'

'I'm enjoying it,' Bridget told her. Of course she was enjoying every minute! 'It's nice seeing everybody. Though I'm to be mainly a spectator myself.'

'Well, you're looking very pretty, Bridget,' the elder girl said and glanced slyly at the man. 'Isn't she, Mr Ledoux?' She was a nice girl and she genuinely liked Bridget Sinclair, but she was intrigued.

71

'Very,' Ledoux said quietly and as Effie with a smiling nod moved away, sat down again. 'What were you doing in Edinburgh, Bridget?'

'Working,' Bridget said promptly. 'In a bank. It's the same bank as Mr Fraser's.'

'I wondered — why they'd taken you to hospital so far away. You were in Edinburgh when you took ill?'

Bridget nodded. 'I really live there now. I stay with Aunt Frances, my mother's sister. I just get back to Achinlaig for holidays.'

'And now I think your mother said you're here for two months.'

'Yes. My bank have given me leave of absence.' Bridget looked rueful. 'I have to try to be sensible about it.'

'Yes. I think you are sensible,' the man said quietly. He smiled, 'I thought you were going to be a schoolgirl. I suppose because it was always Mrs Sinclair's young daughter, young Bridget and so on.'

Bridget's eyes twinkled again. 'I

know. I think years and years ago there was someone else called Bridget in the village so I was known as young Bridget. And it's stuck. How long have you been here?' she asked.

'In Achinlaig — five weeks. In Scotland since November last year. I'm over here for a year.'

'Then do you go back to Canada?'

'That's the plan. But — ' he looked at her seriously, 'I'm to be in Achinlaig for nearly three months yet.'

'Canada must be very beautiful,' Bridget murmured. 'Tell me about it. Whereabouts is your home?'

They went on talking quietly during the rest of that dance and through the interval, and when the next dance began, with a loud and persistent beat, looked at each other and smiled, and then sat back, perforce, to listen.

Several people came to speak to Bridget, others waved as they passed in the dance, and as it was finishing Mary Fraser came and joined them. She sat down on Bridget's other side.

'Everything in trim,' she said with satisfaction. 'Now I can have a few minutes to see who is here. You all right, Bridget?'

'Oh, yes,' Bridget said happily. 'I'm enjoying myself.'

Ledoux leaned forward. 'Mrs Fraser, I've told Bridget I'm taking you two home tonight. I have the car with me.'

Mary looked surprised. 'Well, that's good of you. But — ' she went on saying what Bridget had not found words to say. 'What about your partner? She won't want two other women tagging around,' she added candidly.

It was Ledoux's turn to look surprised. 'I haven't anyone with me. At least — ' he smiled at Bridget 'if I'd known Bridget was well enough to come I'd have asked to be allowed to bring her.'

'Oh, I thought — ' Mary's glance wandered across the room to where the girl in the red patterned dress was dancing with a younger man. Ledoux followed her gaze.

'Oh, you mean those two,' he said easily. 'Robinson I think they call them. They're staying in the hotel, a brother and sister. They were coming out as I was and I just gave them a lift down.'

'That's fine then,' Mary said. 'By then I'll be glad I don't need to walk that mile home.' Ledoux, she decided, must have a young sister back in Canada, as he was taking such care of Bridget.

But the small band was tuning up for the next dance and Mr MacMillan who was middle-aged and the village school-master came up at that. He said he was pleased to see Bridget among them again and asked her to dance. Bridget who would much have preferred to stay where she was, got up and went with him.

Mary chuckled. 'Poor Bridget. She'll not want to waste her precious dances on him. He used to teach her. What about you, Mr Ledoux? Aren't you going to dance?'

Ledoux smiled. 'I will, if you will

have this one with me.'

Mrs Fraser laughed. 'That wasn't what I meant. But yes, I will.' She rose with him. 'Though what all these girls angling for a dance with you are going to say to me, I don't know.'

The young man looked at her a little quizzically. 'I'm not on the market, Mrs Fraser.'

'No?' Mary looked at him with interest and asked her usual direct question. 'Someone back home?'

'No,' Ledoux answered but did not elaborate. He guided her into the centre of the room and looked over her shoulder to where Bridget appeared to be listening earnestly to what her partner was saying to her. At least the school-master's style of dancing would not tire her, and he had to remember that Bridget might not want to spend her whole evening with him.

But when the dance ended Bridget being returned to her place at the same time as Mrs Fraser and Ledoux arrived back, said a polite Thank you to Mr

MacMillan and sat down again happily on the vacant seat between the other two. But not this time, for long.

'Hello there, Bridget!' Ian Watson was a fair young man, whose father farmed in the district and Bridget had known him all her life. 'Glad to see you back home.' He smiled at her audaciously and gave a sideways look at the man beside her. 'It's time someone else had a dance. We can't let the outsider monopolize you like this. Come along, Bridget, my turn.' He grabbed her hands and pulled her out of her seat.

Bridget reddened and momentarily tried to hold back. 'What if I don't want to, Ian?'

'Of course you do,' Ian laughed and put his arm round her waist. 'You were always good at this one.'

Bridget, with her training as the minister's daughter behind her knew she could not refuse to dance with him without giving up dancing for the rest of the evening — and she still had one dance she wanted to have. 'Well, I'm not up to anything strenuous yet.'

'Oh, you'll be all right,' Ian said cheerfully. 'I'll keep hold of you and swing you around.'

'I was wondering when Ian was going to show up,' Mrs Fraser said amiably.

Ledoux glanced at her and frowned. He had heard young Watson, who must be of an age with Bridget, described as the only eligible bachelor left in the district. Bridget had not looked particularly pleased to be so unceremoniously dragged onto the dance floor, but then how could he know yet what Bridget wanted. He frowned still more as the music swept into one of the wilder highland dances. For a few moments he watched sombrely.

'Bridget isn't up to this sort of dance,' he muttered. 'What the hell does young Watson think he's doing! Hasn't he got any sense!'

Mary gave him a quick surprised look, but she too looked along the room to where Ian Watson was swinging Bridget round and round, throwing her from him to catch her and twirl her round even faster. The girl's face was scarlet and she looked, Mary thought worriedly, like a little doll. 'Oh, she shouldn't be dancing like that! Mrs Sinclair wouldn't want that.'

'I bet she wouldn't!' Ledoux stood up. 'I'll go and see if I can rescue her.'

Mrs Fraser gave him a curious look. Ledoux was certainly taking his self-imposed duties to Bridget seriously, but she thought no more of it. She was concerned for Bridget and she sat forward, watching anxiously.

Ledoux, making his way quickly down the side of the room, did not know how he was going to do what he intended to do. He had no desire to create a scene and young Watson might resent him interfering. Bridget herself might not want to come out of the dance because he told her to. But he could not stand by and see her make herself or be made ill in this way. So rescue her he would and in another moment he had done just that literally.

Ian, making another of his spectacular twirls and flings threw Bridget from him. Her feet went from under her, she was falling backwards when the Canadian, still a yard to so away, moved with his long stride and caught her. A smaller man would have gone down too with the force of her falling, light as Bridget was, but he held her, steadying her.

Bridget was gasping for breath, her eyes were closed. She had felt her heels slide, her body falling, expecting to hit the hard floor and now — She opened her eyes and looked at the dark face of the man who was holding her firmly but with gentle hands.

'Stay still, Bridget,' he said quietly. 'Get your breath back.' He was looking at her with such tenderness that Bridget's heart which had been pounding, seemed now to be beating wildly for another reason. But in a moment she wondered if she had imagined that look, for Ledoux's face was stern as he looked beyond her.

'That wasn't clever, Watson,' he said severely but quietly. 'Bridget isn't up to that sort of dancing yet. Couldn't you see that?'

Ian looked abashed. He had got a bad fright when he had seen Bridget falling backwards. 'Sorry, Bridget,' he muttered. 'I forgot.'

There were several people crowding round and Mrs Macleod was saying of course Bridget should never have been expected to dance like that tonight. 'Are you all right, Bridget?' she asked anxiously.

Bridget smiled and nodded. Her breathing was easier.

'Take another minute, Bridget,' Ledoux said easily, 'then I'll take you back to your seat.' He glanced about him and there was a sudden gleam in his dark eyes. He knew what he could do and do easily, but perhaps he had better not.

Bridget was looking about her shyly now. She was not used to being the centre of interest. 'I'm all right now,' she smiled. 'I've got my breath back.

Sorry for spoiling your dance, Ian,' she gave the young man a brief smile, and looked up again at the man who still held her.

'Right,' he said, 'I'll take you back.' He moved but kept one arm firmly about her shoulders as he guided her back up the room. Mary Fraser gave a deep breath of relief as the girl sat down beside her.

'My, Bridget, I was worried there. That was stupid of Ian! I thought you were down.'

Bridget smiled at the man at her other side. 'I would have been if it hadn't been for Mr Ledoux.'

'I don't know what your mother would have said to me if that had happened.' But Mrs Laurie was signalling from the doorway and Mrs Fraser, saying she must be wanted and telling Bridget to sit still for a bit, hurried off.

Bridget turned to the man beside her. 'Thank you,' she said gratefully. 'I really thought I was going to go right on to my back.' She smiled ruefully.

'That wasn't being sensible, was it?'

'Not your fault, Bridget.'

'I don't know how you managed to be there just at the right moment.'

Ledoux raised an eyebrow. 'I was coming to try to break it up.' He looked at her quizzically. 'I nearly picked you up and carried you back to your seat. But I guess that would have caused quite a sensation.'

Bridget coloured prettily, but she laughed. 'It certainly would!'

'Feeling all right now, Bridget,' Ian Watson had come up to them and was asking anxiously.

'Yes, thank you,' Bridget answered. 'I've got my breath back.'

Ledoux stood up. 'I'll go and see if I can get hold of a drink for you, Bridget,' he said. 'Don't move.'

He went off and Ian looked after him. He looked puzzled. 'I didn't think you'd even know Ledoux, Bridget.'

'Mr Ledoux drove my mother and me from Inverness on Tuesday when I came home,' Bridget said simply.

'Oh! What about another dance later, Bridget? A quieter one?'

Bridget shook her head. 'I'm sorry, Ian. I promised to ration myself to four dances and I've had three. And I've promised the fourth one.'

Ian grinned. 'I get it! You're looking very pretty, Bridget. I think I'm going to try and cut him out.'

Bridget looked startled and blushed. She was glad that Mr Ledoux was not there to hear that silly remark. But he did come back at that, said a brief casual word to Ian, who went off, and handed Bridget a glass as he sat down beside her again.

'Lemonade,' he said. 'That's all they have at present. Later I believe we'll get some coffee.'

Bridget accepted her glass and took a drink. 'It's refreshing.' She smiled. 'Lemonade for you too?'

Ledoux grinned. 'Suits me at present. Nothing stronger here as you know. Though some of them do bring it in. Including,' his glance went down the hall to a group of young men whom Bridget had already decided must belong to the Forestry team, 'some of my fellows.'

Bridget followed his look, saw that people were taking their partners for the next dance. 'You have been very kind,' she began.

'Have I?' Ledoux looked at her quickly.

Bridget blushed and shook her head a little. 'I'm really trying to say that — you don't have to stay with me if you want to dance. I know it is delightful for me but,' she went on earnestly, looking at him seriously, 'I'm quite used to sitting watching on my own. So — if you want to dance?'

Ledoux shook his head and smiled. 'I don't. You see it's delightful for me too, Bridget. Later, when you're rested and when they come up with something of a slower tempo we'll have that dance you promised me. And the next time Mrs Fraser has one of her dances I'll bring you and we'll dance every dance. And show them all.' There was a gleam in his dark eyes. 'Meantime I'm very content. Unless,' he raised his eyebrows, 'I'm keeping you away from someone else you want to talk to.'

Bridget shook her head and looked at him shyly. Perhaps he was tired. After all the kind of job he did could not be said to be an easy one. 'Have you been working today?' she asked.

'Yes. We went on till after six. And the last three nights since I saw you on Tuesday we've worked till about eight. Very satisfactory. Making up lost time. Do you like forests, Bridget? Trees?'

Bridget smiled and said she did.

Presently Ledoux got up to return their glasses and when he came back the band was starting to play again.

'This sounds all right. Shall we, Bridget?' He held out his hands to her.

Bridget gave him both her hands and went with him with complete confidence. They did not speak at all until the dance was nearly finished.

'Shall we go outside for a few minutes?' Ledoux said then. 'Get some air?'

'Yes,' Bridget agreed. 'Some fresh air would be good. It does get stuffy in here by this time.'

He guided her to the entrance and looked down at her. 'Now I don't want you to get cold. What about a coat?'

Bridget shook her head. 'I won't need a coat. I expect it is still warm outside. I thought it was hot when Mary and I came along.'

Ledoux stepped outside. 'Yes, it's still warm.' He put his arm round her shoulders again and they walked slowly along the wooden veranda which fronted the hall. There were several other couples doing as they were doing and they walked past them to pause beside the rail. It was a beautiful night and they looked down beyond the dark road to the glimmer of the sea. There were a few lights on the neck of land and on the dark horizon a yellow light which moved.

'A trawler perhaps,' Bridget murmured.

'Yes. Or a naval vessel. It is very beautiful here, Bridget. Each morning I seem to see fresh colouring when I look at your lovely bay. Beautiful tonight too.'

'So many stars,' Bridget said quietly looking up at the thickly scattered sky.

'Yes. Which one shall we have? Choose one, Bridget.'

Bridget laughed softly. 'That one,' she said.

'Right. From now on that's ours.' Ledoux smiled. He bent his head. 'Let me mark it so that I'll find it again.'

'Will you be able to pick it out when you get back to Canada?'

'Yes. When you're in the mountains, in the high Rockies, the stars are so close you feel as if you could reach right up to them.' He took a deep breath. 'I'll show you, Bridget.'

He looked down at Bridget now and saw that she was looking up at him a question in her big eyes. His arm tightened about her shoulders and he looked quickly behind him. The music had started again a few minutes before and the other couples had drifted back into the hall. They were alone.

He looked at Bridget again. There was something he wanted to do, something he knew he was going to do, a question to which he needed an answer. He bent his head and his mouth was on hers. At first it was a gentle kiss, questioning, searching and then as he felt the response of her soft lips, his mouth tightened, his other arm went round her, holding her to him. He raised his head slowly and looked at her, waiting for her reactions with an anxiety he had never known. If she laughed and made of it some light and expected thing, if she went coy on him and slapped his face —

But Bridget had no wiles. She was trembling, looking up at him with surprise and a question in her dark eyes.

Ledoux moved slightly, but his arm

about her shoulders tightened. 'Bridget,' he began. But he got no further.

'Mr Ledoux,' a woman's voice called. The man turned quickly but he did not take his arm from Bridget. 'Oh, there you are!' Mrs Fraser was coming towards them. 'Could you come, Mr Ledoux?'

'Trouble, Mrs Fraser?'

'Brewing, I think,' Mary said. 'Those young ones from round the point and some of your men.' She peered beyond him. 'Oh, it's just you, Bridget,' she said in relief. 'I was afraid I was breaking something up.'

Ledoux's eyebrows went up and there was a brief flash of humour in his eyes as he glanced at Bridget. He took his arm from her shoulders and gripped her hand. 'Right. Lead on, Mrs Fraser.'

As they reached the entrance they heard the raised voices even over the sound of the band and Ledoux, with another brief look at Bridget, released her hand and strode quickly down the room to the knot of people gathered there.

'He'll soon nip it in the bud,' Mary said comfortably. She looked at the girl. 'You're looking better now, Bridget. You've got a pretty colour. Enjoying it?'

'Fine,' Bridget said and smiled.

Mary nodded and went back to her behind-the-scenes duties. Bridget moved slowly on the fringe of the dancers until she reached her seat. She sat down, looking down the hall, watching Ledoux as he talked, as he put a hand on one young man's arm, as he said something to another. So that was what Mary had meant when she said he was useful. He was taller than any of them she thought with a sudden rush of pride and then bit her lip. For what had he meant, what had he been going to say to her? She saw the group begin to break up, the men taking their partners for the next dance and looked away quickly.

This time he might not come back to her. He might know now that she was a silly girl who took seriously a kiss given at a dance. She must not look towards him and if he did not come back she would know that she had been wrong, that he had not meant what her heart was telling her he did mean. She looked at her hands and then tried to pretend an interest in the passing dancers.

Ledoux sat down beside her and Bridget turned quickly to look at him, her heart beating rapidly. For he had come back. But he was sitting forward, his elbows on his knees, his hands clasped, and not looking at her.

'Bridget,' he said so quietly that only she could possibly hear. 'I won't do it again — until you want it too.'

'You think I might want it too?' Bridget whispered asking for an answer as much from herself as from him.

Ledoux smiled slightly and moved his head as if in doubt, in disparagement of himself. He turned and looked at her. 'I hope so, Bridget,' he said sincerely and Bridget met his straight look, her eyes bright, her mouth warm and tender, and knew a sudden and glorious certainty. For a moment they looked at each other and it was she who looked away, who remembered that they must not look at each other like that in this crowded room, where someone was sure to be watching them.

Ledoux sat back and gave her a quick understanding grin. 'Sorry,' he said. 'I forgot.' He glanced at his wristlet watch. 'It's nearly eleven. This evening has flown. I think I'd better go and see if I can get hold of that coffee for us now, Bridget.'

Bridget smiled. She, too, thought the evening had flown. 'Shall I come too?'

'No. You stay here. There'll be a crush there now. I'll bring it back here and we'll have it in,' his eyes twinkled, 'more or less, peace.'

He returned a few minutes later, carrying two mugs of coffee and precariously balancing a plate of sand-wiches with two sausage rolls on top. 'Better grab that, Bridget, before we lose them all together.'

Bridget laughed as she took the plate from him. 'Oh, Mary's sausage rolls. She was worrying on the way here in case they hadn't arrived.'

'Well, they are in great demand and I nearly lost those two on the way up.' He handed her a mug of coffee and sat down. 'I'm hungry. Aren't you?'

'Yes.' Bridget was surprised to find she was. 'This is fun. A picnic supper.' She looked at him happily.

'Then I think we're going to have a lot of fun together,' Ledoux said quietly.

When they had finished Bridget went back with him to hand in their used dishes to where Mrs Fraser and her helpers were finishing clearing away. 'This next one will be the last dance, Mr Ledoux,' Mary called from behind a counter.

'Is it? The usual waltz, I suppose.'

'Of course,' Mary said.

'In that case — ' Ledoux smiled at Bridget, 'and as you aren't going to walk all that way home — ' He held out his arms to her and she went into them without question. And though he held her as gently, as firmly as he had done for their first dance, their second dance, both knew that it was now entirely different.

When it finished there was the usual rush for coats and for cars. Bridget, having retrieved her coat, stood waiting for Mrs Fraser while Ledoux went to bring his car to the front. Mary joined her in a few minutes.

'Is Mr Ledoux still taking us home?'

'Of course,' Bridget said. 'He's bringing the car. Here he is now.'

They went down the steps and Mary was just getting into the front and Bridget into the back when a gay voice said, 'Hello there! Haven't you forgotten me?'

Ledoux, one hand on the door turned. His eyebrows came together. He wondered why he had been expected to remember her. Though he rarely even noticed the admiring glances which came his way he was no fool.

'Did you want a lift back?' he said quietly. 'Where's your brother?' He glanced behind her.

'Oh, he's deserted me!' Moira said tragically.

'Right. We'll give you a lift,' Ledoux said in a matter-of-fact tone. 'Miss — er — Robinson, isn't it? Mrs Fraser. Miss Sinclair.' He made the introduction in the same brisk tone and shut the door after Moira had joined Bridget in the back.

The two girls looked at each other.

'I hope you enjoyed the dance, Miss Robinson,' Bridget said politely. She would rather have walked the short distance to the hotel than done that, she thought. Some men, of course, liked girls who threw themselves at them. She remembered what her mother had said on Tuesday about the visitors to the hotel, and smiled as she looked at the back of their driver's head. For her mother had been wrong about him. She knew that. She had no doubt.

'Oh, not bad.' Moira threw back her long hair. 'These village hops are all the same, don't you think.'

Bridget smiled but did not answer and Ledoux's car was already pulling into the forecourt of the hotel and stopping.

'Oh, you didn't need to stop specially for me,' Moira said gaily. 'I'm not in a hurry.'

But Ledoux had stopped. 'That's all right,' he said and turned to watch as she got out, starting up again as soon as the door was shut.

Mrs Fraser chuckled. 'One disappointed young lady,' she murmured.

'What?' Ledoux frowned. He hoped that Bridget did not think — 'We'll take Bridget home first, Mrs Fraser,' he said quietly and took the car down the hill and past the Bank house to pull up in front of the manse. This time he got out, opening the door for Bridget, going to open the gate for her.

Bridget called goodnight to Mrs Fraser and then looked up at him.

'Thank you for bringing me home,' she said softly.

He smiled. 'Our star is still shining.' He lowered his voice, 'Bridget, you know what is happening between us, don't you?'

'Yes,' Bridget whispered. They looked at each other for a moment and then with a soft, 'Goodnight,' she went on up the path.

Ledoux stood watching while she opened the front door and then went back to his car to swing it round and back up the hill to the Bank house.

In the hall Bridget paused, took a deep breath and went towards the living room where there was a light and where she knew her mother would be waiting for her.

Morag put down the newspaper she was reading and smiled. 'Had a nice night, Bridget?' She looked critically at her. But Bridget's eyes were bright, she had a pretty colour in her cheeks and she did not look tired. So maybe she had taken no harm.

'Very nice,' Bridget replied sedately, and thought how inadequate that sounded. But her wonderful dream was too new, too precious, too dreamlike to be shared with anyone.

'Did you get a lift home? I thought I heard a car?'

'Yes.' Bridget could not keep back her warm smile. 'Mr Ledoux brought us down.'

'Ledoux?' There was a wariness in Morag's eyes. 'Mary, too, you mean?'

'Of course. He was to drop her on the way up again.'

So Bridget had not been alone with him. That was something. 'Well, you don't look any the worse for your gay night, thank goodness. Did you have some dances?'

'Yes. Four. No,' Bridget remembered and corrected herself, 'Five.' She waited for her mother's next question.

But this time Morag bit it back. As Ledoux had brought them home no doubt he had felt he had to ask Bridget for one dance, but she must not make too much of it. 'Do you want something to eat, Bridget? A hot drink, maybe?'

'No thank you, Mother. I had some supper.'

'Well, in that case, we'd better get away to bed. Morag stood up and shook up the cushion on the chair. 'Or else we'll have your father complaining that we're falling asleep during his sermon tomorrow.'

'We mustn't do that,' Bridget said lightly. She followed her mother up the stairs, whispered goodnight and went to her own room. She was pleasantly tired, but she was not going to sleep for a long time. She had too much of which to think, to remember, to feel. For she had never been in love before. And he — Her hand went to her mouth in sudden dismay, but her eyes laughed. Oh, how silly she was! For even yet she did not know his christian name.

4

Bridget listened to her father announce the text for his sermon and dutifully found the place in her bible. Behind her she heard the slight rustling as people settled back in their seats in the tiny church. When she and her mother had arrived, there had not been many in their places but by now she knew it would be full. She put down her bible on the ledge in front and leaned back, looking up at the minister, but truth to tell, seeing him not at all.

Though morning had brought a touch of reality to her dreams, a wonder as to why he even liked her, she still had the deep and certain conviction that it was not merely her own girlish dream. This was something which belonged to them both. He had said so. And he had shown her so. For there had been no reason why he should have stayed with her the whole evening if he had not wanted to do that. She bent her head quickly to hide the sudden flash of amusement in her eyes. For never before had Bridget had the undivided attention of one man at a dance, and she was quite sure that not only she but everyone there had noticed that. That knowledge would be quickly passed around to everyone who had not been at the dance, including, of course, her mother. This morning her mother, surprisingly, had again omitted to ask with whom she had had her dances, contented herself with asking what some of the other women were wearing. When Bridget had looked blank and could not tell her, she had shaken her head indulgently. Her mother, of course, did not like him but once she got to know him properly as she would do now, she would like him.

When and where would she see him again? That he would make the opportunity she did not doubt. She went on dreaming and when her mother rose for the last hymn got hastily to her feet, knowing guiltily that she had not heard one word of her father's sermon.

A few minutes later the minister came down from the pulpit to go to the entrance, and Bridget paused in the aisle behind her mother as Morag stopped to say a few words to old Mrs Campbell who sat in the opposite pew. Bridget's look went beyond her mother, her eyes widened, her colour mounted. Ledoux, moving with the crowd at the back of the church towards the doorway, was looking towards her. He smiled and Bridget smiled back happily. So all the time he had been behind her. But her mother had moved on, there were others crowding into the aisle and her view was blocked.

She had never expected him to be in church. For at the back of her mind, and it had stayed there, had been the thought that there might be a difference in religion which might provide difficulties. But he had been there. Surely she should have sensed that! Would she see him when she got out or — for he was well in front — would he be on his way up the road.

She smiled at her father as she passed him in the porch and as her mother stopped to speak to Mrs Macleod skirted them and went down the short path. For Ledoux was standing at the edge of the road, he was alone and he was watching — he was watching for her. She reached him.

Ledoux looked down at her with an eager scrutiny. 'How are you, Bridget? All right after last night?'

'Perfectly all right,' Bridget smiled. He was looking at her exactly as he had done last night.

'Everything,' he put a slight emphasis on the word, 'O.K.?'

'Everything,' Bridget said, her eyes bright. 'I had no idea you were in church.'

Ledoux smiled. 'I had the advantage of you. I've been admiring your cute hat. But don't tell your father that.'

'I won't. Have you been here before?'

'Sure. I'm now one of the minister's regular attenders. What do you do for the rest of the day, Bridget?'

'Father has an evening service at a wee church about five miles away — he goes there once a month. But — ' But before Bridget could say that she did not think she would be going too, Morag had reached them.

'Good morning, Mr Ledoux,' she said sedately. 'I'm hearing we're indebted to you again.' And as she saw the surprise on the young man's face went on, 'You were kind enough to run Bridget home from the dance last night.'

Ledoux smiled warmly at Bridget. 'I wouldn't put it that way, Mrs Sinclair. I hope you didn't think last night tired Bridget too much.'

Morag looked at her daughter's bright face and in all honesty could not say so. 'Och, I don't think she took any harm.' She looked at the man and hoped that was true in all ways. 'I'll see she gets a rest this afternoon and an early night tonight.'

But already the brief interlude was over. Old Mrs Cameron had come up to Bridget, was asking her how she was; Mrs Sinclair had turned to speak to another couple, and Bridget, while she answered the old lady heard Mr Laurie saying, 'I'll walk up with you, Mr Ledoux. You were asking me about — ' She heard no more but she turned her head.

Ledoux, separated from her now by not only her mother but several others, gave her a rueful lift of his eyebrows, and Bridget returned his look. After all of what use to expect to have any private conversation surrounded by all the rest of the congregation. It was not as if they could have walked home together, for home, for her, was here.

A few minutes later, following her mother up the path to the manse she thought wistfully that it would have been nice if her mother had renewed her invitation to tea on Tuesday which he had been unable to accept. For apart from her own wishes, he had done them a good turn on Tuesday, and today, she was sure, he would have accepted. But her mother, apparently, had had no such thought.

On the Monday Bridget spent most of the day pulling the gooseberries which were now thick on the bushes at the bottom of the garden at the back of the manse. After that they had to be topped and tailed and put ready for the jam making the following day.

After tea, as she had a letter for her aunt to post, Bridget walked along the road to the post office. It was a fine warm night, and she did not hurry, pausing every now and then on her way back to look out over the bay, to mark the silver trail of a fishing boat, and the distinctive mountains of northern Skye. It was going to be a clear night again. She must look out to see if she could see the stars again, to see one particular star. She smiled to herself as she walked on and did not see the tall man walking with long strides across the machair which separated the road from the stretch of yellow sand and the sea.

'Bridget,' he called and she turned then quickly, her colour rising. Ledoux was coming swiftly down the slight hill, jumping the crevices, taking the last section with a sliding run which brought him to her side.

'Bridget!' He looked at her eagerly, searchingly, marking her colour, her bright eyes. 'How are you now? I think — you do look much better than you did last week.'

'Oh, I am!' Bridget's smile was warm, for he was looking at her with a tenderness she could not mistake, just like that look which she had thought she had imagined on Saturday night. Everything was as she had known it was. They looked at each other for a long moment.

'Have you been bathing?' Now Bridget's mouth had a tender curve for she realized that at last she was seeing him in one of those gay shirts which her mother disliked. She thought its vivid checks of orange and red and green were absolutely right. He was carrying a towel and his thick black hair was shining with the wet. 'Was it very cold?'

He smiled. 'Yes. Too cold to have asked you to join me. I sometimes manage a swim at night, if we aren't working too late. But always in the morning.'

'In the morning? What time?'

'Before you should be up. Six to seven generally. I looked to see if you were in your garden as I came along, Bridget, but no.'

'I've been to the post office,' she said. She remembered something. 'What is your name?' she asked. She saw the sudden dismay on the man's dark face. Did he think she meant she had even forgotten who he was? She smiled warmly and went on quickly and with a confidence she had never known. 'Your christian name. I don't know it. And it's so silly to have to go on thinking of you as Mr Ledoux.'

'Ross,' Ledoux said and took a deep

breath. He gave a little shake of his head. 'That was stupid of me. Of course no one here will have ever heard it. Ross Ledoux,' he said again and gave her a little bow.

'Ross,' Bridget repeated. She liked it. It suited him. 'R-o-s-s?' she spelt it and looked her question.

'Yes,' he smiled. 'I have a French-Canadian father and a Scottish mother. Now what other facts ought you to know?' He considered. 'I'm twenty-nine. Single. Unattached — till now. Six foot six according to my passport,' he grinned. 'How old are you, Bridget?'

'Twenty-one. But I'll soon be twenty-two. But — only five foot three I'm afraid.'

'Just perfect. When is your birthday, Bridget?'

'The thirtieth of September.'

'Two months. So that when your two months convalescence which your mother said you had to have are up you'll be twenty-two.' He gave a little nod. 'We'll have to make that the target. I'm the fourth of January. Then I'll be thirty. So that makes it seven years — nearer eight. Just about right, I think.' He raised his brows and gave her a warm caressing look which made Bridget's colour deepen. 'What do you think, Bridget?'

'Just right, Ross,' Bridget agreed and for a moment they smiled at each other in complete understanding. Then slowly they began walking up the road.

'I think that covers the basic facts,' Ross said. 'We'll need to discover other things gradually. The little things — like do we or do we not take sugar in our tea — and how much.' He gave her a laughing glance.

Bridget laughed happily too. 'Or eat our porridge with sugar or with salt!'

'There I go wrong. I know it. My mother always declared it should be eaten with salt though, mind you, she is always ready to spoon on the maple syrup herself. You, I suppose, being a good Highland Scot, take it with salt?' One eyebrow went up.

Bridget's eyes twinkled and she hung her head in mock shame. 'With sugar!'

Ross laughed. 'That makes two of us!' He put out his hand and took hold of hers, enfolding it warmly. 'It's a beautiful night, Bridget.'

'Oh, it is,' Bridget said rapturously.

But an old woman was coming slowly round the corner they were approaching and as she reached them she stopped. 'Why, it's the little Bride!' she exclaimed. 'How are you now, lassie?'

Bridget stopped too, smiling at her. Old Mrs MacDonald lived in one of the fisherman's cottages beyond the post office and now she had to be told in detail how Bridget was after her illness. Ledoux had released her hand and walked on and as Bridget talked to the old lady, answered her questions, asked after her health and listened to details of the last letter she had had from her son who was now in Australia, she was wondering if Ross had gone straight on up the hill. For they were not out walking together, this was just a casual meeting — She should have known better of course for when Mrs Mac-Donald had gone slowly on and the girl turned there was Ledoux waiting for her a few yards up the road.

He was looking at her seriously as she reached him. 'Why did she call you Bride?' he asked abruptly.

'In the Gaelic Bridget is Bride,' she told him. She smiled at him lovingly as she saw the swift relief on his face. 'Mrs MacDonald always calls me Bride.'

'Does she?' Ross gave her a rueful grin and she saw again that slight shake of his head which she was coming to know. 'I thought you'd given some other man the right to call you that.'

'No,' Bridget said simply.

'No one in Edinburgh, Bridget?'

'No one.'

His look was serious. 'Unattached, Bridget?' and as she nodded, added softly, 'till now?' There was a shy but wonderful light in Bridget's dark blue eyes as she nodded again. Ross took a deep breath and then, 'Did they christen you Bride?' he asked.

'Oh, no,' Bridget said fervently. 'Thank goodness for that! Think what a handicap that would have been.'

'Would it?' He looked amused.

'Of course! Imagine! You're a spinster of sixty and everyone calls you Bride!' She laughed gaily. 'I was saved from that.'

Ross laughed too. 'I see your point. But that isn't going to happen to you.'

Bridget smiled at him happily. 'Both my sisters got Gaelic names,' she told him. 'Catriona and Sheena.'

'One of them lives in Glasgow, I believe.'

'Yes. That's Sheena. She is married to a minister too. Catriona lives in England, in Portsmouth, and she has a little girl. Then there's Dave. You know Dave.'

'Yes. I've met him.'

'Do you have brothers and sisters, Ross?'

'No. I'm the only one.'

But walking slowly as they were,

stopping every few yards just to look at each other, even they could not make the short distance to the manse any longer. They had rounded the last bend and were passing the church. In the manse garden David Sinclair, busily hoeing one of his borders, heard his daughter's laugh, a man's deep voice and looked over the low wall. Who could Bridget be talking to, for that did not sound like her at all. He stared. Young Ledoux. And Bridget, who had always hung back behind her mother or her sisters, who had been too shy to talk to any young man, even those she had known all her life, seemed to be having plenty to say to this one. And the big man was walking slowly at her side, bending his head to watch her as he listened, as he talked to her.

The minister looked amused. When had this happened? Not certainly on the journey from Inverness on Tuesday according to Morag. He glanced towards the house, but his wife was not at any of the windows. What was she going to

115

say about this? But hadn't she said something about Ledoux driving Bridget and Mary Fraser home from that dance on Saturday? And yesterday, after the service, he had noticed that Ledoux, contrary to his usual habit of walking straight away from the church, had been hanging about outside the gate. Hoping to see Bridget, perhaps?

His eyes twinkled, but the two were reaching him now and he straightened and smiled at them both. 'A beautiful night, Mr Ledoux. Bridget, your walk to the post has given you quite a colour.'

'I think she looks much better already, Mr Sinclair,' Ross was giving Bridget a look of possessive affection which was not lost on her father.

'I'm sure she is,' he said and smiled affectionately at his daughter. 'Are you just coming back from your work now, Mr Ledoux?'

'No. We finished quickly tonight. I've been for a swim.'

'Ross has a swim every morning

between six and seven, Father,' Bridget put in.

The minister's eyelids flickered. So he was Ross, was he, and Bridget had discovered that. 'Well, he's young and energetic,' he laughed.

'You're being energetic yourself I see, Mr Sinclair,' Ross smiled. 'You have a fine display of colour in your garden. I suppose you are quite sheltered here?'

They talked garden for a few minutes then Ledoux said Mr Sinclair would want to get on with his work so he would say goodnight. He looked at Bridget and said a quiet 'Goodnight, Bridget' to her.

Bridget smiled at him. 'Goodnight, Ross,' she said and stood a moment beside her father until Ross had disappeared round the bend of the hill before turning to go up the path to the house. Her father looked after her. So he had been wrong. Strange things did happen, even things as strange as this. This was what Morag had feared. And though he knew nothing against the young man, he knew very little about him. And Morag, with her mother's instinct might be right. They would need to watch it.

In the house Mrs Sinclair was just crossing the hall as Bridget entered. She had heard voices and thought she detected a trans-atlantic accent in one of those voices.

'Did you meet someone, Bridget?' she asked casually. 'I thought I heard voices. Who was it?'

'It was Ross, Mother,' Bridget smiled.

'Ross?' her mother repeated. 'Who is Ross?' She was asking a genuine question.

'Ross Ledoux,' Bridget said and her voice as she said the name had a lilt in it. 'His christian name is Ross.'

Ross indeed! Morag's mouth thinned. 'It may be,' she said primly, 'but I'd have thought it hardly fitting for you to use it.'

Bridget coloured. 'Why not, Mother? Is he — is he very important or something?'

'Ledoux? Of course not! I meant,' she hardly knew herself what she had meant, 'he's a stranger here, and you're just a young girl.'

Bridget relaxed and smiled. It was just her mother's way. 'Well, we aren't strangers now.' Her eyes twinkled. 'He had on one of those shirts you admire, Mother! Orange and red and green checks.'

Despite herself Morag smiled. Now she was on sure ground. 'Now you'll see what I meant when I said they were hideous.'

Bridget laughed and shook her head. 'I liked it,' she said stoutly. 'Absolutely gorgeous. Mind you,' she went on gaily, 'I was beginning to wonder when I was to see one of those gay shirts. For on Tuesday he had on a green one, on Saturday a white one and Sunday it was blue.' She turned and went off up the stairs, leaving her mother staring after her, astonishment mingling with dismay on her face.

For this was Bridget, who had been

unable to tell her what any of the other women had been wearing at the dance, but seemed to know the colour of every shirt she had seen Ledoux wearing. She did not mean it, of course. For some reason she was being perverse. She was too much like herself to like a man like that.

Why had that car had to break down just on that particular day? For this, of course, was what she had feared would happen. Bridget, who at one time would have shied away from a man like Ledoux, now felt she had to be friendly with him, and because she was grateful, pretend to like him. And the young man too, no doubt, had similar thoughts. For David had been right there. Bridget was certainly not the type of girl who would attract him. She was too quiet, too gentle, too — too much of a lady. She was worrying for no reason. For after all, these had all been chance meetings. If Ledoux were ever to try to get Bridget to go anywhere with him, if he were to go out of his way to try to see her, then that would be time enough for her to start to worry.

She did not have long to wait for the very next afternoon while she was busy with some sewing in the drawing room which looked to the front she heard the knock on the front door. David had just gone to the small room he used as a study to start on his next Sunday's sermon and Bridget was busy in the kitchen. Morag got up to answer the door, glancing from the window as she did so. There was a grey car standing beyond the gate, its bonnet pointed away from the village. She stiffened. Ledoux's car. He might, of course, be wanting to see the minister. She crossed the small hall and opened the door.

Ledoux was in his working garb, with his trousers pushed into high boots, and his shirt of red and green checks open at the neck. He smiled. 'Good afternoon, Mrs Sinclair. Is Bridget in?'

'Good afternoon, Mr Ledoux,' Morag said soberly. 'Come in, will you,' she stepped back automatically, holding the door for him to enter for she was the minister's wife and no visitor to the manse was ever denied admittance. 'Bridget — ' she hesitated. 'Will you come in here?' she moved to the living room door.

Ross, having stepped into the hall as she shut the door behind him, stood still. 'I'll not come any further, Mrs Sinclair. I'm on my way back to the camp.' With his goal straight before him he went on, 'I've to go into Inverness on Thursday and I wondered if Bridget would like to come in with me.'

'Oh, I don't know about that, Mr Ledoux.' Mrs Sinclair shook her head. 'The journey there and back would be too tiring for her. It's kind of you to offer — '

But Bridget, busy at the kitchen sink, had heard the voices and hastily dried her hands. She came into the hall, smiling warmly. 'Hello, Ross.'

The young man's eager look went beyond Mrs Sinclair to Bridget as she came forward. 'Hello, Bridget. I'm just telling your mother I've to go into Inverness on Thursday and I hoped you'd like to come in with me. She thinks it might be too tiring for you.'

'Why, thank you, Ross. I'd love to come with you.' Bridget's blue eyes sparkled. Had she not known that he would make the opportunity for them to see each other? And how handsome he looked, how tall. She heard her mother give a little cough and looked at her. 'I won't be a bit tired, Mother. After all I've been making jam all morning and I'm not a bit tired now. And I'll be sitting in the car nearly all the time.' She looked happily at Ross. 'And you and I both know what a comfortable car Ross has.'

'Oh, aye, I know that.' Morag tried for lightness, 'But I'm thinking I'll need to remind you that you're supposed to be convalescing, my girl. For it won't be just the ride there and back. Mr Ledoux will have his business to attend to and you'll soon get tired walking about the town.' For a moment she wondered if she should say that she would go into Inverness with them. That would serve two purposes for she would be able to keep an eye on Bridget and at the same time show Ledoux that she did not take his offer to drive Bridget as being any different to his offer of last week to drive them both. But Thursday was certainly not a convenient day.

'I'll enjoy seeing the shops,' Bridget was saying. 'After all, it's a long time since I had a good shop-window gaze.'

'Well, I don't know — ' Morag began doubtfully. She looked from one to the other, at the big man standing quietly waiting — what was he thinking, what was behind this? — at her daughter's bright face. Surely David was not already so immersed in his sermon that he had heard nothing! Why did he not come and help her to get out of this? For he, just a day or so ago, had been worrying because Bridget looked so frail, so pale. She gave a sigh of relief as the door of the room opposite opened and the minister came out.

'I thought I heard voices,' he looked about him. 'Good afternoon, Mr Ledoux.'

'Mr Ledoux is saying he's to go to Inverness on Thursday, David,' Morag began quickly, 'and he's kindly offering to give Bridget a lift in if she wants to go. But I'm saying it would be too much for her yet, don't you think so?'

'Oh, I don't know, Morag. A day out will do her good.' He smiled at Bridget, 'Do you want to go, Bridget?'

'Yes. I've just accepted Ross's invitation.' Bridget looked at Ross and saw from the slight smile he gave her that it was an invitation and not quite the way her mother had put it.

'I'll take very great care of her, Mrs Sinclair,' he said then, and the minister at least heard the sincerity in his voice even if his wife did not.

'Well then,' Morag gave in reluctantly. 'If your father says so, Bridget. Are you aiming to leave at nine o'clock again, Mr Ledoux?'

'Nine o'clock will do if that suits Bridget.'

'I could make it earlier, Ross,' Bridget smiled. 'I know you are an early riser.'

'Eight-thirty then. We can stop on the way for coffee and break the journey for you. Thursday morning then, Bridget.'

'Are you having a long day today, Mr Ledoux?' David asked as Ross took a step back to the door.

'Yes, we're working late tonight, tomorrow too. We're aiming to give ourselves a full day off next week, as we didn't take a holiday on Monday.' Again Ledoux's look went to Bridget who was walking across the hall to the front door as he opened it.

Mrs Sinclair gave her husband a meaning look. So Bridget was to share that holiday, was she? They would have to see about that. But maybe after one day in his company Bridget would have realized that they could have nothing in common. No doubt that was why David had been willing for her to go on

126

Thursday. Morag had great faith in her husband's judgment.

'Good afternoon, Mrs Sinclair,' Ross called as he went out of the door. 'Eight-thirty Thursday, Bridget,' he said again and smiled at her.

'Yes,' Bridget agreed happily and watched him go down the path to his car. She waved, stood till the car went round the bend and then went back into the house. Her father and mother were both still in the hall. She smiled from one to the other. 'Oh, I do hope it's fine on Thursday. Mother, I'll bring you some of those shortbreads. You did say you wished you had some more. Didn't you say there was a book you wanted, Father?'

'Yes, I'll give you a note of it.' The minister looked at his daughter with affectionate amusement. 'Now what do you think of the young man's shirts, Bridget? Agree with your mother?'

Bridget laughed and shook her head. 'Of course not! Lovely!' Her eyes twinkled at her mother. 'I think Mother is just pretending she doesn't like them.'

'I am!' Morag was horrified. 'Not a bit of it! I never did like loud colours. Nor did you, Bridget,' she looked accusingly at her daughter. 'Why you would never wear such colours yourself.'

'That's different. I don't suit bright colours. But Ross — he's dark and handsome, so he can wear and look splendid in striking colours. I'll away and get finished.' Bridget moved to the kitchen leaving her mother to make an expressive face at her husband.

The minister was laughing as he followed Morag into the living room. 'What a change the last few days has made in the child!'

'Aye. I knew she'd be all right once she was home,' Mrs Sinclair said complacently. 'But — do you think she'll be all right on Thursday?'

'Of course. Do her good to get away on her own.'

'But — with Ledoux?' Morag was

still doubtful. 'All those hours — alone with him. At least four hours, two there and two back.'

David was looking at her with amusement. 'Well, Morag, I hardly think he'd have come and given us notice if he'd been intending an immoral assault.'

'David! What a thing to say!' Morag smiled reluctantly. 'Notice indeed!'

'That's what you have in mind, isn't it?'

'Of course,' Morag admitted. 'A man like Ledoux! And Bridget is so innocent.'

The minister shook his head. 'I doubt if Bridget is as innocent as you think, Morag. And,' he paused and went on seriously. 'I'm wondering if she hasn't a better judgment of people than you and I. As for the young man, well, I'd have thought he was behaving very correctly — coming asking your permission before he takes her out.'

'Aye, maybe,' Morag admitted. 'No doubt he just thinks he's doing us a good turn by giving Bridget a lift.' She brightened. 'And after an hour or so with nothing to say to each other — you know how shy Bridget is — they'll discover they have nothing in common.'

5

'Now, Bridget, don't forget to go to that café and get yourself some lunch.' Mrs Sinclair gave her daughter a meaning look as she walked with her down the path to where Ross Ledoux had just stopped his car. 'You'll need tidying,' she lowered her voice.

'Yes, Mother,' Bridget's eyes twinkled. She smiled at Ross who had got out of his and was standing holding open the front door for her. 'Hello, Ross. It's a lovely morning.'

'Sure is,' Ross smiled from her to her mother. 'I'll have her safely back by about six o'clock, Mrs Sinclair.'

'Six?' Morag repeated weakly. What on earth were they going to do all that time? But Ross was shutting the door after Bridget and going round to get into the driver's seat. Bridget called good-bye to her mother and Ledoux put up his hand as he started his car. Before Mrs Sinclair could think of anything to say it moved away.

'Oh, it is a beautiful day.' Bridget leaned back happily. 'Last night it seemed to be clouding over and I was afraid it was going to rain.'

'It cleared late on. Our star was shining so I knew it was going to be all right.' Ross smiled but did not take his gaze from the twisting road in front of him. 'What was that your mother was saying about lunch, Bridget? I thought you were going to have lunch with me.'

'I'd like to,' Bridget admitted, 'but — will you have time? Will your business be finished?'

'I haven't a great deal to do today. Sometimes I have to give a talk, but not today. So I should be through by one o'clock if you can wait till then.'

'Of course. Do you give talks, Ross? About forestry?'

'Yes. Not quite my favourite occupation, talking. But — that's partly why I'm over here. Exchanging ideas.' They had left the shore behind them and were taking the winding road inland. He pointed to the track which led away into the forest. 'That's where we are working now,' he told her.

'Is it?' What are you doing, Ross? Felling the trees?'

'A few of them. Not many. Just those which should come down. Because they are diseased. Over-planted. Wrongly planted. This is a well-grown forest, so we're going through it, checking, repairing as it were.' Ross gave her a swift glance. 'Would you like to come and see what we're doing some time, Bridget?'

'Oh, I would! Could I?'

'I'll take you,' he promised.

Bridget leaned sideways in her seat, looking at his dark strong profile, his big work-worn hands on the wheel. There was a warm light in his eyes. 'I think your job means a great deal to you, Ross,' she said gently.

'I suppose it does,' Ross admitted slowly. 'I never wanted to be anything else. My father is a lumberjack, so all my life I've spent in the forests. I think my parents had the idea that I might want to branch out a bit, do something entirely different. But no. So when I went to college, to university, forestry was still my goal. After all in our country it plays a major role. And there's plenty to learn, plenty of new ideas coming up.' He gave her a rueful smile. 'But maybe it's just because I like working in the open air, with my hands, among growing things.'

'I think to be a forester,' Bridget said slowly, 'not only must you like the quiet things, but you must have an awful lot of patience.'

'There's that,' Ross admitted. 'You can't expect results this year, even next year. And,' he grinned, 'you've got to be tough and brawny, like me. But you, Bridget, what do you like? You've been in Edinburgh for four years. Do you want to go on living in a city? Would you be bored living in the country again?'

'Oh, no! I could never be bored in the country. I like it best. Of course I like going to the town sometimes. For a few days. Or for a day's shopping like we're going today. I enjoy that. But I like to look out at mountains and lochs and — ' she hesitated and then went on with confidence, for though she could not think of why anyone as splendid as Ross should like her that he did she could not doubt, 'like you I love trees and woods and quietness.'

'Were you born in Achinlaig, Bridget? Do you mean you want to go on living there?'

'Not particularly in Achinlaig,' Bridget answered quietly. 'Yes, I was born there. We all were. Were you born in Quebec, Ross?'

'No. In Ontario, actually. Miles away from anywhere. Father and mother were living there then. I suppose,' he hesitated and went on slowly, 'that was why I was baptized in my mother's church and not my father's. Not that he is in any way dogmatic or particularly religious. Nor am I. To be candid I can't say I've attended many church services until I came over to Scotland last year. I had my first four months in Invernesshire and I got friendly with the minister of the small church there. So I started going.'

Bridget smiled. 'And continued.'

'Yes.' Ross gave her a quick serious look. 'So no problems there for us, Bridget,' he said quietly.

'No.' Bridget's look was equally serious. 'I did wonder. Not that it would have been a problem.' She flushed realizing just what she had said, how much she was taking for granted.

But Ross was accepting it without question. 'No,' he agreed, 'it wouldn't.' He pulled his car into a parking place, acknowledged the salute of the oncoming driver and then moved away again. 'We did have about eight years in Quebec province after that,' he told her. 'Away in the wilds of course. It's fine country as you'll have to see. Then my father got a job right at the other side of the country, in British Columbia, and they've been there ever since. That's where I was working before I came to Scotland — about two hundred miles north of where they are. And where there's a job waiting for me when I go back.' He smiled. 'It's a grand country, Bridget. I've got to sell it to you within the next two months.'

'It sounds wonderful.' Already Bridget knew he would have no difficulty in selling her his country.

'It is. But this is wonderful too. The views alongside Loch Maree and looking back from where we are now. Marvellous colouring.'

'Yes. Where were you before you came to Achinlaig, Ross?'

'In Sutherland. I was there during spring and early summer.'

They went on talking as the car took them away from the loch and over the long stretch of moorland. Despite what Mrs Sinclair had thought and perhaps hoped they found no difficulty in talking to each other. Bridget had completely forgotten her natural shyness and asked questions with ease; they were finding out how much they did have in common.

Soon after ten when the long barren stretch was behind them they stopped to have coffee. It was then that Bridget asked, 'How did you get the scar on your cheek, Ross?'

Ross laughed. 'An axe head which came adrift. It happened when we were very far away from proper facilities so that is how I was left with this.' He looked at her seriously. 'It can be very lonely, Bridget. Particularly during the winter days. You have to live your own lives, make your own entertainment.'

'I think some people can be lonely anywhere, even in a city.' Bridget said quietly. She took his coffee cup from him, and refilled it. 'It depends upon the kind of person you are, who you are living with, what you want from life.' She smiled. 'I'm sure your mother, even though she lived in all those far-away places was never lonely in that way.'

Ross laid his hand briefly on hers. 'You're a wise child, Bridget,' he said quietly. 'Yes, mother always seemed to fill her time in happily. And they both enjoyed reading, father in particular. He passed that on to me. Do you like reading, Bridget?' Then, as she nodded, he smiled and went on, 'Of course everything is much easier now, even in the most isolated settlements. Better facilities, lighting, heating. And you can fly into a city for a few days quickly and quite easily.' He took a drink of his coffee and glanced at his watch.

'Should we be getting on again?' Bridget asked.

'In a few minutes. I want to find time to get my hair trimmed. I've got to try and look respectable when I take you out to lunch.'

Bridget's eyes twinkled. 'I had my hair cut short when I was in hospital. I used to wear it to my shoulders, but I'd have been having it shortened in any case. Long hair is all right when you're very young, but when you get older it looks out of place.' She caught Ross's look of amusement and broke off. 'Are you laughing at me, Ross?' she asked suspiciously.

His smile widened. 'Shall we say, just a little bit? Twenty-one! Never mind.' He put his hand out and let a tendril of her hair curl round his finger. 'I like it. Just as it is.'

Bridget had a pretty colour in her cheeks as she shook her head slightly. Ross took his hand away slowly.

'Now I suggest you go and find the ladies' room while I pay the bill,' he said easily.

Bridget went off, smiling as she remembered her mother's last anxious words, knowing that with any other man she herself would have been awkward and shy, but with Ross everything was so easy, so natural. She had known this was going to be a lovely day and it was. It was!

When they reached Inverness Bridget had her leisurely look in shop windows, shopped for the things she wanted to

get, and was wandering along Queens-
gate in good time for her meeting with
Ross on the corner, when he caught up
with her, as she was pausing beside a
shop window.

He put an arm about her shoulders
and smiled down at her. 'Bridget.
Finished your shopping?'

'Yes,' Bridget smiled back at him.
'I've had an enjoyable browse around.'

'Good.' He took her shopping bag
from her and put into it the oblong flat
parcel he carried. 'For you,' he said.
'Chocolates. I don't yet know the kind
you prefer, but I do know you can't tell
me not to buy you any because you're
on a diet.'

'Why thank you, Ross! I'm sure to
like them,' she assured him. She gave
him a critical look. 'Smart,' she said
judiciously.

He laughed. 'Tidier, shall we say.' He
took hold of her arm. 'Come along. By
now, we are both hungry.'

They went on, paused beside a
jeweller's window, where he showed her

the kind of brooch set with a topaz, which he had sent over for his mother's birthday the previous month, then moved to a window of records, where Bridget was pleased to discover that Ross liked music as she did.

'I've a catholic taste,' he told her, 'but with a preference for real music. You, too, Bridget?'

'Yes. Aunt Frances and I used to go to a concert occasionally — in Edinburgh. I liked that.'

'They have concerts in Vancouver.' He smiled as they went on.

In the hotel where he took her for lunch they had a corner table and they enjoyed and lingered over their meal. Bridget had a look at her chocolates, showed Ross the book she had got for her father, and was told by him that he had got his business completed satisfactorily.

'August seems to be a slack time for headquarters — holidays I expect. So I won't be expected to come in for anything next week.'

'Are your team taking summer holidays this month, Ross?' It had just occurred to Bridget that Ross himself might have plans to go off somewhere.

'No — apart from the odd day that is. When this stint is over we'll all have a break. Meantime we get as much done as we can during the long days.'

'They don't mind working long hours?' She relaxed again happily.

'No. They like it that way. Plenty of overtime. For none of them have homes in the district. For the older married ones it's mainly work and sleep and save their money for a longer holiday between jobs. Some of the younger ones go off to Inverness at the weekends occassionally for a night on the town.' He gave her a straight look. 'I'm past that stage, Bridget.' He smiled. 'But I am planning to take a full day off next week, and I hope you're going to share it with me. Are you?'

'If you would like me to.'

'You know I would. What would you like to do?'

'What would you have done if you hadn't met me?'

'Found you,' Ross corrected. 'Oh, just had a day's fishing on my own. Take my lunch and my tea and go off to some really isolated loch and do nothing — just fish. I'd do that at home too.'

'You're a keen fisherman? Of course!' Bridget smiled. Had she not known at the very first that he was a quiet man. 'Then let us do that, go fishing. There's good fishing around Achinlaig.'

'I know. But — that would be very dull for you.'

'It wouldn't! A lovely, lazy day in the open air. I'd keep count of the fish you catch. I'd enjoy that.'

'Would you? Really?' Ross looked so pleased, so eager that Bridget knew she would have gone with him even if it had been the last thing she wanted to do. But just to be with him would be enjoyment for her.

'I would. That's what we'll do, Ross. Shall I bring a picnic?'

'No. I'll take that. The hotel will put up something for me. They're quite good at that. Wednesday, I think, Bridget. But I'll come to the manse and ask you properly, so that I have your mother's approval. I don't want her to think that I'm persuading you to do anything which she thinks might give you a setback.' He smiled at her warmly. 'I don't forget you're still convalescing after that illness. But before we get to Wednesday I'll see you on Sunday.'

'After church,' Bridget's eyebrows lifted.

Ross grinned. 'Most unsatisfactory that. Too many people wanting to talk to you. But what about the evening? Does your father have a service somewhere to which you have to go?'

'No. That's just once a month. I didn't go on Sunday.'

'Did you not?' Ross looked rueful. 'I thought — but, of course, your mother said you were tired after the dance.'

'I wasn't a bit tired,' Bridget said

stoutly. 'Mother goes with him but father has never expected all the family to go too.'

'I missed out there. I was going to ask if I could take you for a drive. So — what about this coming Sunday? Would a drive on a Sunday evening be permissable for the minister's daughter?'

Bridget laughed. 'Quite permissable. Father isn't sticky, Ross. In some places, in the islands for instance, you daren't do a thing. But in Achinlaig more than half the congregation come to church in their cars, and father and mother often go out themselves on a Sunday evening.'

'Then — Sunday evening?'

Bridget agreed happily. They finished their lunch, went into the lounge and sat for a long time over their coffee, then started off on the homeward journey.

'We'll take it slowly,' Ross said. 'I thought we could stop at Kinlochewe and have tea there, so that will get us back just about six, as I promised your mother. I've got to see that I get a good mark for today.' There was a teasing light in his dark eyes as he took hold of her arm.

Bridget's smile was warm and loving as she assured him that he was certain to get that.

At about the same time Mrs Sinclair was in the store at Achinlaig. She had driven David to a farm he wanted to visit and then made a few calls herself. There was a meeting of the Ladies' committee, to decide on their autumn activities, to arrange for before Mary Fraser went on holiday the week after next, and Morag had decided on next Wednesday afternoon. Now she had her last call to make on Mrs Macleod, to see if that day suited her as it did all the others. She stopped her car and went into the store. Yes, Wednesday would be fine for her, Mrs Macleod agreed and Morag gave a little nod of satisfaction. She had several ideas ready to put forward, and now that Bridget was at home she could make the tea and bring it into them, so that her mother would not have to leave the other ladies.

'There are a few things I'll take when I'm here, Mrs Macleod,' she said and was packing them into her basket when Effie Cameron came in. The younger woman greeted the other two cheerfully and then asked, 'How is young Bridget now, Mrs Sinclair?'

'She's improving greatly since we got her home,' Morag answered and hoped that no one asked where Bridget was today.

But Effie was going on, 'My, I got a shock when I saw her first on Saturday night. But she perked up fine later, as well she might, mind you.' She laughed gaily. 'Made quite a sensation on Saturday, did Bridget. Didn't she, Mrs Macleod?'

Mrs Sinclair had stiffened. 'A sensation? Bridget?'

'She certainly did. Gave us all a surprise when she made such a conquest. Good for Bridget. One young woman from the hotel was literally green with envy.' Effie missed the warning faces Mrs Macleod was pulling at her, but saw Morag's look of cool enquiry. 'Mr Ledoux,' she explained gaily. 'Devoted himself to her the whole night. I've never seen that young man give any girl more than one dance, and I'd have said he was strictly a safety-in-numbers man myself. But not on Saturday.'

Mrs Sinclair's smile was frosty. 'Mr Ledoux? Well now the young man did give me a lift in to Inverness and drive Bridget and me out again, as you'll remember, Mrs Macleod. And I'm sure he has some manners, so, of course, he'd speak to Bridget. And Bridget,' she gave a light laugh, 'she's always been a polite child so — ' She paused meaningly, hoping by those few words to have shown how wide was the gulf between her daughter and a man like Ledoux. 'Effie and her exaggerations! For I know Bridget only had a few dances.'

'Oh, I'm not saying she danced all night,' Effie said cheerfully. 'She was very good there. I think, yes,' she had been keeping count, 'she only had three dances with him, but he sat out with her all the rest of the night, he got her supper for her, and he was nicely on hand to rescue her when she nearly went on to her back through Ian Watson playing the fool. If that isn't — ' She broke off.

Mrs Macleod had at last caught her eye. 'And very glad we all were that Mr Ledoux was there to catch Bridget,' the older woman said severely. 'She'd have gone down with a nasty crack if he hadn't. Ian should have had more sense, trying to make Bridget dance in that wild way.'

Morag was startled now. 'You mean Bridget had a fall? I've not heard of this.'

'No, no,' Mrs Macleod assured her. 'Mr Ledoux saved her from that, he caught her as she was falling.' She smiled. 'He's a big lad. Bridget couldn't knock him over.'

'Couldn't she?' Effie said saucily.

Mrs Macleod smiled. 'Ah, well, you're only young once. And I'm sure they both enjoyed themselves. It didn't do her any harm, did it, Mrs Sinclair?' she asked anxiously.

'Not at all.' Morag was cool again. She asked Effie a question about her husband and got off the subject of that unfortunate dance. But when, a few minutes later, she got back into her car and started away up the hill, her mouth was tight. It was too bad of Bridget, getting herself talked about like this. If she had spoken to Ledoux and had had one dance with him that would have been all that was necessary. And had Mary Fraser seen nothing of all this going on. Surely she would have told her. Of course Effie Cameron was given to gilding the gingerbread. She had already made one call on Mrs Fraser this afternoon, but she would call again now.

Mary looked surprised as she opened

the door. 'Oh, won't Wednesday do after all?'

'Yes, that's fixed.' Morag stepped in. 'I just wanted to ask you what happened at the dance on Saturday.'

'The dance? Oh, it went off fine. We made seven pounds and twenty-three pence, and that's very good for an August dance.'

Morag smiled slightly. Mary always saw the practical side first. 'I mean — what happened about Bridget? I've been hearing such a tale from Effie Cameron.'

'Bridget?' Mary's brow furrowed. 'Oh, you mean when she nearly fell. That wasn't her fault. Ian Watson dragged her into one of those wild dances and started flinging her around. Mr Ledoux and I were both worried about her. He said you wouldn't want her to be dancing like that. Mind you, she'd have had a nasty toss if she had gone down, but he caught her as she lost her balance.'

'Ian? Or Ledoux you mean?'

'Ledoux. Ian looked a bit ashamed.'

'According to Effie there was more to it than that. She said Ledoux stayed with Bridget the whole evening.'

'He did,' Mary admitted. 'I think he must have a little sister like Bridget back home, and was just keeping an eye on her.'

Mary, of course, with her matter-of-fact approach made it all sound quite different. 'You think that's all it was?'

'Oh, yes.' She caught her friend's doubtful expression. 'You don't think he's taken a fancy to Bridget do you?'

'I hope not,' Morag said sedately. 'But Effie seemed to think — '

'Oh, Effie!' Mary said scornfully. 'You know what a chatterbox she is. Why I'd never have thought of such a thing.' She laughed heartily. 'That big man! Why he'd crush her with one hand.'

Mrs Sinclair shivered delicately. 'I know. Of course it's foolish. But — if you hear any gossip, scotch it, Mary, will you?'

'I will,' Mary agreed cheerfully.

She would not say anything to David, Morag thought, as she went on to the manse. He would just tell her again that she was worrying unnecessarily and laugh at her. But she would have a quiet word with Bridget. She had always been an obedient child, ready to do anything to please her mother. Having been so long in Edinburgh she must have forgotten how people talked in Achinlaig, how even a small courtesy could be magnified. And also, of course, what was expected of the minister's family —

Mr Sinclair had not returned to the manse when Ross drew his car up to the gateway and got out quickly to come round to Bridget's side. He put both hands out and lifted her out bodily, holding her a moment, smiling down at her as he steadied her on her feet.

'Oh, I've had a lovely day, Ross,' Bridget's colour was bright as she smiled back at him. 'Thank you very much for taking me.'

'Thank you for coming with me, for sharing the day with me.' He reached into the back of the car for her bag.

'You'll come in, Ross?' Bridget said.

'No. Not tonight. I'll just come up with you to hand you over to your mother.' His eyes twinkled and Bridget laughed gaily.

'I must be a parcel,' she said as she led the way up the path.

Mrs Sinclair, in the sitting room, heard the car stopping but as she hurried to the hall and the door, missed seeing the mode of her daughter's alighting. She opened the front door as they reached it.

'So you're back,' she said unnecessarily. 'Will you come in, Mr Ledoux?'

'Not tonight, Mrs Sinclair. I've a few notes to make when I get back.' He put Bridget's bag into a corner. 'I just wanted you to see I've brought Bridget back safely. And not tired at all, I think.' He gave Bridget a teasing smile.

'Well, we're grateful to you for taking her, Mr Ledoux. I hope she wasn't any trouble to you — you with your business to do!'

Ross laughed. 'Oh, a great deal of trouble, Mrs Sinclair. I had great difficulty in seeing she didn't do all the things she hasn't to do.'

Morag, whose sense of humour was not her strong point, looked startled but not displeased. If that were so that might be the end of this.

'Ross Ledoux!' Bridget pulled a laughing face at him and gave her mother's arm an impulsive squeeze. 'He's teasing you, Mother. Oh, we both had a lovely day.'

'Of course,' Ross smiled at her lovingly. 'Sunday then, Bridget. Good-night, Mrs Sinclair.' He went back down the path putting up a hand to Bridget as he got back into his car and moved away.

Morag shut the door and followed Bridget into the living room. 'Sunday,' she said. 'What does that mean? At church?'

'We will see him at church, but we're

going for a drive on Sunday evening. We're going to go up to Gruinard Bay. It's ages since I was up that way. Is father out, Mother?'

'Yes.' Her mother looked at her for a moment. She had intended to wait awhile before she said anything, but this — another outing! 'I got a shock when I was in the store today, I may tell you, Bridget. All the talk about you! That dance!'

Bridget looked puzzled. 'Dance? Oh, you mean because I nearly fell. But I didn't, Mother. Ross saved me from that. Mind you, I thought I was going flat on my back — it was an awful feeling. It was Ian Watson, he's a silly young boy.'

'He's as old as you are,' Morag said dryly. 'But that wasn't all I heard. They were talking — and I don't like to have my daughters talked about like that — about you and Ledoux.'

Bridget coloured but she laughed. 'Well, Mother, everybody talks about everybody in Achinlaig, don't they. And

157

they're bound to know. Why not?' She saw her mother's astonished lift of her eyebrows and thought she understood. 'Oh, did you think he might be married or something, Mother. Well, he isn't.'

'He told you so, I suppose,' Mrs Sinclair said tersely.

'Of course.' Bridget gave her mother an impulsive hug. 'It's all right, Mother. Ross and I we — ' she hesitated for to her mother she could not use that word which she used in her own thoughts, 'we like each other — we like each other very much. Oh, we get on fine. I had such a lovely day.' She moved to empty her shopping bag. 'Look what Ross bought for me.' She produced the chocolates. 'Gorgeous, aren't they?'

Morag cleared her throat. 'I don't think — ' she began but got no further. They heard the front door open and the minister's quick step across the hall.

He smiled from one to the other as he came in. 'Back are you, Bridget?' He looked about him. 'Ross not here?'

'No, he didn't come in,' Bridget answered.

David gave his wife an enquiring look but she did not meet it. He picked up the box of chocolates from the table and his eyes twinkled at his daughter. 'My, what it is to have a young man who can afford to buy you this sort of thing. When I was courting your mother she was lucky if she got a bar of chocolate.'

'I expect she was pleased with that too,' Bridget said stoutly.

'I was that,' Morag admitted, but she gave her husband a look of exasperation. Young man, indeed. It was too bad of David. Bridget, it seemed was going to need no encouragement to fancy herself in love with Ledoux.

'Had a good day, did you, Bridget?' her father was asking.

'Oh, a splendid day,' Bridget said enthusiastically. 'There's your short-breads, Mother.' She took them out of her bag. 'And I got your book, Father. They had it in stock.'

'Good girl.'

'Ross likes reading.' Bridget gave a little laugh. 'He reads much more serious books than I do. He's reading some Scottish history just now.'

'Is he?' her father smiled. 'I'll have to have a talk with him about that.'

'Yes.' Bridget picked up her basket and moved to the door. 'I'll away upstairs.'

'He's taking her out for a drive on Sunday night she tells me,' Morag said heavily as soon as they heard Bridget's step on the stairs.

David, already dipping into his book, looked at his wife. 'Is he? That'll be nice for her.' he smiled. 'My, it's good to see Bridget looking so happy, so lively. When we think of what she was like when we went down to see her in hospital, even what she was like when she came home last week.'

'Yes,' Morag agreed slowly. She paused, looked at her husband and then decided to say nothing. 'I'll away and see to the supper.' David could not be blind, but probably he thought it was something which would pass. She would have to try and think that too. She would have to hope that some glamorous young woman came to stay at the hotel, so that Ledoux would no longer want to bother with quiet, gentle Bridget Sinclair.

6

When the service finished on Sunday morning Bridget went past her mother as soon as she stopped to speak to someone and quickly threaded her way down the path to the road, where she could see Ross waiting for her. He smiled, 'Come for a walk?' he said.

'Now? But — ' Bridget glanced behind her.

'Five minutes. Quickly down the bank and back again,' Ross said. 'They'll all be gossiping for longer than that. And you must let me take a walk with that hat.' He held his hand out to her and Bridget, laughing, put her hand in his and went with him.

A minute later Mrs Sinclair, coming down the path, stopped to speak to Mrs Laurie and then looked about her. 'Where's Bridget? Where has she got to?'

'Oh, she's just away for a wee walk,' Mrs Laurie said comfortably. 'With her young man.'

Morag stiffened. Bleakly she looked down the road. Yes, there was Bridget. But surely she was not walking hand in hand with Ledoux? It was too bad, with everyone seeing them like this! She smiled frostily, 'Oh hardly that, Mrs Laurie. It is just Mr Ledoux.'

Mrs Laurie smiled indulgently. 'I'm thinking you'll maybe be having another wedding at the manse this year, Mrs Sinclair.'

There was a spot of colour in Morag's cheeks. 'I sincerely hope not,' she said firmly. 'I'd enough with Sheena's wedding last year.' It was as well that Bridget had not been there to hear that remark, putting silly ideas into her head. She turned with relief to speak to someone else.

A few minutes later she raised her eyebrows at her husband as he followed her into the house. 'She's away walking with that man,' she said indignantly.

'Who?' David looked at her vaguely, but comprehension brought a flash of amusement to his eyes as Bridget came up the path.

'I've been having five minutes air and exercise,' she said lightly.

The minister smiled at her. 'You're not so lucky as we were, Bridget,' he told her. 'When I walked your mother home from the kirk it was a mile even if we took the direct road. And if we took the long way over the golf course, we could make that stretch a very long way.'

'Tush!' Morag said and pursed her lips as she went to take off her hat. Why did David persist in making comparisons with something which could not be compared. But she was glad Ledoux had seemingly gone straight on back to the hotel. She hoped he did not come in when he came for Bridget tonight. There was no knowing what David might say, what wrong impression he might give to the young man.

But Ross Ledoux, despite the fact

that he had been about the world, despite his outward appearance, was in essentials as simple and straightforward as was Bridget herself. He knew what he wanted, knew now that Bridget wanted it too. But Bridget was younger than he was, she had about her an aura of innocence which he recognized, she had been brought up in a sheltered and close family. So, because he too had spent most of his life in small communities, not only Bridget's parents, but the whole of the village, had to be left in no doubt as to his intentions. For himself he would not have cared one way or other what anyone said. The sometimes malicious gossip, the inevitable innuendoes would pass over his head, and eventually everyone would know what he meant. But he did not want it that way for Bridget, his gentle, sensitive love. Above all her parents had to be shown that their young daughter would be safe with him, that he was ready to, and could take proper care of her. For Bridget, despite the fact that the improvement in her health since she came home to Achinlaig was noticeable was still frail, still at times looked like those delicate windflowers to which he had at first likened her. And he did intend to take her a long way away from this home of hers. That her family might look at him askance because of that he recognized. That they would look at him askance for any other reason did not occur to him. Materially he could provide for her, and provide for her well. He was doing well in his chosen career, he had every intention of going further.

So when he arrived at the manse that evening and Bridget opened the door for him, he followed her into the sitting room where both David and Morag were sitting reading their newspapers.

'Good evening, Mr Ledoux,' Mrs Sinclair greeted him in her usual polite cool fashion. 'You're taking Bridget for a wee run I'm hearing.'

The minister was not so formal. He took off his glasses and smiled. 'Hello,

Ross. Where are the two of you off to tonight?'

'We're going up to Gruinard Bay.' Ross smiled from one to the other. 'It's such a fine night the colouring should be good.'

Bridget had lifted her coat from the back of the chair where she had laid it. 'I don't think I need to put on my coat,' she said.

'There may be a cool breeze from the sea, so you'd better put it on.' Ross took it from her and held it for her to put on. Bridget gave him a laughing glance and obeyed.

Her father's eyes twinkled. 'Have you been working this afternoon, Ross?' he asked.

'No. Not on a Sunday,' Ross answered. 'I have a lazy afternoon, reading the Sunday papers and writing my weekly letter home.'

In that case, David wondered, and looked pensively at his wife, why had Morag not asked him to have tea with them. There had never been any lack of

167

hospitality when the other girls were courting. In the year before Catriona was married he was sure Hugh Murray had spent much more time at the manse than he had in his own home. And last year Sheena had seen to it that Tom came up to stay for at least two nights every week.

But Ross was going on, 'We've caught up now on the time we lost through the wet weather last month. We're all taking a full day to ourselves this week. Bridget is going to share mine with me.'

'What are you planning to do?' David asked before Morag could do more than look aghast.

Ross gave Bridget a quick grin. 'We're going fishing.'

'Fishing?' Morag found her voice. 'Why Bridget has never fished in her life.'

Bridget laughed merrily. 'Ross is going to do the fishing. I'm going to keep check on his catches.'

'I won't be allowed to get away with

any fisherman's tales you see, Mrs Sinclair.' Ross smiled at the elder woman. 'If this weather continues I hope that will be all right for Bridget.' He raised an interrogative eyebrow. 'It won't be tiring for her, and I'm borrowing a couple of rugs from the hotel for her to sit on. They'll pack me a lunch and tea too. And, of course, if the weather does change, we'll do something else.'

'Well, I don't know — ' Morag began slowly. Ledoux, she thought dryly, had covered all the small objections which sprang to her mind before she could even voice them — the weather, the dampness of the ground — She did not realize that Ross saw himself as her ally where Bridget's health was concerned, that he credited her with the same singleness of purpose there as he had himself. But Morag was seeing other objections, a whole day and completely alone — with Ledoux! But how to object without saying that outright —

But David was saying calmly that

that would be good for Bridget, nothing like fresh air and sunshine, and was Ross keen on fishing, did he fish in his own country. Ross answered him, telling him where he was going on Wednesday, the fish he caught in the lakes among the Canadian Rockies.

'When is this to be?' Morag asked then. 'Which day?'

'Wednesday,' it was Bridget who answered.

'Wednesday?' Mrs Sinclair brightened. 'Oh, you've forgotten, Bridget! You won't want to go out on Wednesday. That's the day I've arranged for the Ladies' Committee meeting.' She smiled meaningly at her daughter.

Bridget coloured but looked doubtfully at her mother. What she had to do with the ladies' committee she did not know. In the past her mother had always wanted her daughters to keep out of the way when she was entertaining like that.

It was the minister who laughed heartily. 'I'm sure Bridget will have no difficulty in choosing between the ladies' committee and her day with Ross, Morag.'

'Well — maybe — ' Mrs Sinclair gave her husband a pained look. So she was to have no consideration even from David. Where now were her plans for that nice leisurely tea? And it seemed that David saw nothing wrong in Bridget spending the whole day with a man like Ledoux. She could only hope he was right. She smiled reluctantly. 'What time are you going, Mr Ledoux?' she asked.

Ross answered her and again smiled from one to the other. 'I'm also hoping, Mrs Sinclair,' he went on, 'to persuade you and Mr Sinclair to come and have dinner with me at the hotel next Sunday evening.' He glanced at Bridget. 'Bridget, too, of course,' he smiled. 'Or any other night if you think Sunday isn't suitable.'

'That's very kind of you, Mr Ledoux,' Mrs Sinclair said slowly, but she was even more dismayed. At the hotel Mrs Robertson would see them, everyone would think they were accepting Ledoux. She looked uncertainly at her husband.

But the minister was smiling and accepting with alacrity. 'Thank you, Ross. We'll be very pleased. And Sunday will be fine. My wife and I will enjoy that. Won't we, Morag?'

This time Morag caught her husband's look and knew what was expected of her. 'We will that. Thank you, Mr Ledoux. And you must come in and have some supper with us on Wednesday when you get back from your day's fishing.' She saw the swift pleasure on her daughter's face and bit her lip. The last thing she wanted to do was to encourage Bridget but what else could she do.

'I'll be glad to, Mrs Sinclair. Thank you,' Ross accepted.

'And don't think you need to go home and change first, Ross,' the minister put in cheerfully. 'My wife is used to young men coming for meals in all sorts of garbs.' A minute later he rose and went with Bridget and Ross to the door, watching them as they drove away. He was smiling broadly as he came back into the room. 'Well, Morag, we don't need to have any doubt as to who is making the running here, do we.'

'What?' Morag said cautiously.

'Not like Sheena.'

'Sheena?' Morag bristled a little.

David laughed. 'Now even a fond mother like you can't pretend that Sheena didn't do the running. I'm certain Tom hadn't an idea that he was going to get married until he heard me read out his name from the pulpit.'

Mrs Sinclair gave a reluctant grin. It was a lifelike picture. 'Well, I'm sure they're very happy.'

'Oh, I'm sure they are,' David agreed. 'No doubt Tom, who never could make a decision, needs a wife like Sheena who can. Now this is a different kind of young man altogether. He's made his mind up that he is going to marry Bridget and intends that we should know it.' He caught his wife's expression and gave her a quick grin. 'All right, Morag, you can say I told you so. You were right and I was wrong. Those two have fallen in love with each other.'

'In love? Nonsense, David! They've only known each other for less than a fortnight. You can't really think that?' Far from wanting to be proved right, Morag now wanted to be convinced that she was wrong.

The minister looked at her with amusement. 'Don't you? There's one thing, Morag,' he went on, 'this is the first time you and I are going to get anything out of it. Dinner at the hotel! You'll enjoy that.'

'I don't know,' Morag said slowly. 'It makes it so awkward. Don't you see, David, it'll look as if we approved of Bridget going about with Ledoux.'

Mr Sinclair looked at her seriously. 'There's no reason why we shouldn't, is there? I like the young fellow. It's up to us to get to know him and he obviously wants us to do that. And as I've said before, we know nothing against him.' There was a glimmer of humour in his eyes. 'I've certainly had no irate mothers coming to me to complain about Ledoux.'

'Tush!' Morag said severely. 'He's a foreigner. And he's a lot older than Bridget.'

'Hardly a foreigner. Older, yes, but that's no bad thing for Bridget. She's not a silly child. I'll tell you one thing, Morag, Ross will be able to provide for her materially in a way I've never been able to provide for you. I'd say he was much better off even now than I am, than either of our sons-in-law.'

'He's a French-Canadian,' Morag said severely. 'He may be a Catholic. And you know how many children they have. Bridget couldn't stand that.'

David smiled. 'Young people these days know how to manage that. Even you and I, in our little backwater, know that, Morag. As for his religion, I doubt it. In any event we'll soon find out for I'll ask him.'

'Ask him?' Morag was aghast. 'You can't do that, David! He'd think you were expecting him to marry her.' She took a deep breath. 'He's quite unsuitable for Bridget,' she said firmly. 'Look at him — his hands — Bridget would never want to marry a man like that.'

The minister frowned. 'I don't follow those arguments. What is it, Morag? Have you someone else lined up for her? I hope you aren't trying to do a bit of matchmaking with young Ian Watson.'

'Ian? Of course not!' Mrs Sinclair told him then of what had happened at the dance.

'Silly young fool! But if not him, who else? There isn't anyone.'

'Of course not. No one.' Mrs Sinclair hurried on, 'There is no need for Bridget to get married. She has a good home here. She's always been a home girl. Now that she's here I'm planning to keep her. I could do with her help about the house. It would let me give more time to the parish. And if she got a part time job at the bank — Alec Fraser would be glad to have her — that would keep her in pocket money and clothes.'

'You mean for a month or two — or indefinitely?'

'I mean — for always.'

'No, Morag,' the minister said sternly. 'My dear, we're only in our fifties and Bridget isn't going to be expected to sacrifice her entire life for us. That sort of thing went out before the war, thank God. Bridget will have her chance to make her own life the same as her sisters.'

'But Bridget likes doing things in the house.'

'Yes. Her own house.' The minister was still stern. 'For her husband and her own family.' He smiled, 'I'm sure, Morag, when you think about it, you'll want Bridget to have the kind of happiness we have. As for some help for you, I'm sure we could afford to get someone from the village to come in and help you now that our family are out on their own.'

But that, thought Morag, would not be the same. But she did not say any more on the subject. When David spoke to her in that severe tone she knew he meant it. And if Morag Sinclair valued anyone's opinion it was her husband's. She would just have to hope that Bridget would soon see for herself how unsuitable it was. And if a word here and there from her helped her to see that then that would be the way. Probably having him to the house, letting her go on seeing him, would help to disillusion her too. And Ledoux would surely be leaving Achinlaig soon. He would not be here indefinitely.

When Bridget came back that night she even managed a show of interest in where she and the young man had been. And apart from a lift of her eyebrows, a slightly pained look, made no comment when Bridget arranged her Monday visit to the store to coincide with the time of Ledoux's return to the hotel to collect his mail, when she went out on the Tuesday night about six o'clock, saying casually she was going to meet Ross as he came back from his swim.

Bridget, completely happy in her love and convinced by now that her mother could not help but like Ross now that she was getting to know him, had no thought of being secretive. When Wednesday came and it was a fine morning, with a blue sky and just a hint of haze obscuring the far islands, she was singing as she washed up the breakfast dishes. And when Ross's car drew up she went off to join him waving cheerfully to her mother as they drove away.

They stopped at the store, while Ross went in, coming out with a handful of chocolate bars which he dropped into Bridget's lap. 'To keep us going until lunchtime,' he told her. Bridget laughed and leaned forward to wave to Mrs Macleod, who had followed Ledoux to the door.

They took the twisting, rising road northward for a few miles and then turned off on a narrow rutted track to a spot where they were to leave the car. In front of them a small loch, its waters pale blue in the morning light, lay serenely on the high moors. All around them were the mountains and away on their left hand, stretching away deeply below them, was the length of Loch Maree.

Ross took the rugs and his fishing gear in one hand, and took hold of Bridget's arm with the other, as they picked their way over the tufted, rocky moorland to find a spot close to the loch. The rugs were spread on a flat piece of green grass with a convenient rock for a backrest, and Bridget sat down while Ross went back to the car for the rest of their gear. They were out of sight of the winding road, though they could hear the occasional car as it climbed upwards, and there seemed to be no one else fishing, no one in sight at all. Bridget took deep breaths of the fine air and thought it was a heavenly spot. She smiled at Ross as he came back, putting their things in the lea of the rock.

'Comfortable?' he asked.

'I'm fine. Oh, this is a lovely spot.'

'Sure is.' Ross looked about him. 'Now I'll reconnoitre.' He walked away to the right coming back in a minute. 'It's boggy that way so you're not to go that way.' He strode off in the other direction, disappearing for a moment and then returning. 'Firm round that way,' he said quietly. 'And secluded. So you go that way, sweetheart, when you want to leave me for a few minutes.' He dropped down beside her and began fixing his rod.

Bridget looked at him lovingly. She leaned forward, watching what he was doing. 'I'm getting a lesson.'

The morning went by serenely and quietly. Apart from the distant traffic there was only the occasional harsh cry of a seabird to break the stillness. The sun rose higher, the air grew warmer, the lights on the water deepened, the shadows, the sunlight moved on the mountains. They talked in low tones, they ate their chocolate, they sat quietly. Ross fished diligently but without result. By the time they stopped to eat their lunch he had caught nothing.

'I guess every fish in that loch is on a diet — not a rise have I seen.' He grinned at Bridget. 'Your ability to count isn't being put to much use is it, Bridget. Never mind, we'll see what we can do later. And now, I'm hungry. Aren't you?'

'Ravenous,' Bridget agreed. She laughed. 'For all I've been eating chocolate all morning.' She looked about her. 'Oh, this is perfect, isn't it?'

'Perfect,' Ross agreed. They smiled happily at each other and then proceeded to eat their way steadily through their ample lunch.

Afterwards Ross took some of their things back to the car, while Bridget wandered away for a few minutes. She came back to dabble her hands in a small burn which tumbled into the loch nearby and then settled herself back on her thick rugs. It was hot now, and she leaned back lazily, closing her eyes against the sun.

Ross, busy with his line again, smiled a little as he looked at her. He sent his long line out over the blue water and sat back watching it for a few minutes. He drew it in slowly and looked again at Bridget. Yes, she had gone to sleep. She was breathing evenly, her lashes were dark against her cheeks, the sun had flushed her skin with pink. She looked very young, very fragile, and there was a deep tenderness in the man's dark eyes as he watched her. He resisted the temptation to draw a finger down her soft cheek, for he did not want to wake her. He reached for her coat and carefully spread it over her, he put his own jacket over her legs and her feet. He cast his line again out over the deep water. At that moment Ross Ledoux had everything he wanted from life.

It was nearly two hours later when Bridget opened her eyes. For a moment she stared at the blue sky, at the deepening colour of the water in her line of vision, and then sat up quickly, smiling as she realized how well she had been covered.

'I must have been asleep! Oh, how lazy of me!' She glanced at her wristlet watch. 'Good gracious!'

Ross grinned at her. 'Do you good, sweetheart. Feeling all right?'

'Oh, yes. But how rude of me!'

'Rude. Not a bit of it.' Ross put his hand out now and touched her flushed cheek gently. It was at that moment that he felt the tug on his line and turned quickly. 'Got one, Bridget,' he muttered.

Bridget moved, coming to kneel beside him, watching excitedly as he played his line with skill. 'Oh, it's a big one, Ross.' she clasped her hands tightly as the ripples widened in the water, as the big fish surfaced and fell back.

'Sure is,' Ross gave her a quick boyish

grin as he wound the line in slowly. 'Now, that's a real beauty,' he said with satisfaction several minutes later.

'Oh, it is,' Bridget agreed. 'Worth waiting for, that one, Ross.'

'Sure,' Ross said again and smiled. 'I was beginning to wonder what we would say to your mother if we had to go home without a fish for her.'

Bridget looked at him with bright eyes. 'Mother? Are you going to give it to her?'

'Of course.' Ross was matter-of-fact. 'We'll need to take it to the hotel to have it weighed and checked in. Then we'll take it to your mother. Will she like to have it?'

'She'll be delighted with it,' Bridget said emphatically and had no thought that her mother's delight might be qualified. 'It's a beautiful fish.'

Ross smiled. 'Now, Miss Sinclair, after our energetic afternoon,' he gave her a teasing look, 'we need some tea. What about it?'

'Of course.' Bridget laughed as she

reached for the basket. 'I am hungry again.'

Ross moved to the water's edge to wash his hands and came back to drop down beside her, taking his teacup from her. They lingered over it and then, saying he would call it a day as far as fishing was concerned he began packing away his rod. He stood up. 'I'll go and stow all this in the car.'

'Shall I come?' Bridget looked up at him. 'Should we go?'

'Not yet. There's still heat in that sun.' He looked about him. 'We'll stay till the sun moves behind that peak.' He pointed and smiled at her. 'Then we'll go down to the hotel. For despite what your father said, I must put on a tie and a darker jacket before I come to the manse with you.'

Bridget looked at his bright green shirt. 'I think you look very smart as you are.'

Ross laughed. 'Maybe you're prejudiced, sweetheart.' He gathered up their gear and strode off to the car. He came back with a towel in his hand, bent to splash his face with the water of the loch, and stood smiling at her as he dried himself. He sat down beside her again, putting an arm round her waist.

'It's been a marvellous day,' Bridget murmured. 'And such a lovely evening now.'

'Yes.' Ross took a deep breath. 'What more could a man want? A view as magnificent as this one. Air like this. Quietness. A stretch of water which produces a fish like that one. A day off from his work in which to enjoy it all. And — his girl beside him enjoying it all too.'

'Even though she goes to sleep for hours,' Bridget smiled.

'That's part of it,' Ross said solemnly. 'Are you happy with me, Bridget?' he asked quietly.

'Oh, yes,' Bridget looked up at him, her eyes shining. He looked at her, a long serious look and she, remembering, put up her hand to touch his face where the long scar disfigured it and raised her mouth to his.

This time their kiss was the kiss of two people who loved each other, who knew that in time they were going to give each other much more than that. Ross, feeling the response of Bridget's soft mouth, held her closely but gently for several minutes before he raised his head. They sat then quietly, saying little, supremely content with each other, until the sun moved behind the peak. He stood up then, lifting her, holding her against him for a moment. They went back to the car.

Arrived back at the hotel, Bridget sat in the car while Ross went in to have his fish weighed and to put on a sombre brown tie with his green shirt. He also changed his checked jacket for a plain brown one and when, a little later, he returned to the car, Bridget smiled and told him he looked very smart.

They went on down to the manse. Mrs Sinclair knew what was expected of her as a hostess and on this occasion she was determined to be gracious;

partly because David wanted it that way, but partly because she wished to show her daughter the gulf there was between her and Ledoux. She accepted the gift of the fish with pleasure; after all the minister enjoyed a fish dinner and it was a good and big fish. And if, while they were having their meal she continued to address the young man as Mr Ledoux, Ross put that down to the fact that Mrs Sinclair was more formal than her husband, and Bridget was deciding to ask her mother why she, too, could not call him Ross.

The minister, who had an easy friendly manner, kept the conversation going. He asked questions about Canada, about Ross's job, and was interested in the history in which Bridget had told him Ross was also interested. He was getting to know him and he was sure Morag must be doing the same, discovering that he was a quiet and intelligent and sensible young man. And, of course, he looked from one to the other, very much in love with their young daughter.

'You've caught the sun today, Bridget,' he said lightly. 'Hasn't she, Morag?'

Bridget, in the act of rising and reaching for the teapot, laughed. 'The sun was really hot up there,' she said. Her laughing glance went to Ross. 'I went to sleep.'

Morag went bright red. 'You went to sleep?' she said, a rising note in her voice which Bridget misinterpreted.

'Oh, it was all right, Mother. Ross wouldn't let me get cold. He covered me with the coats. I'll away and refill the teapot.' She went off.

She had not seen either the growing horror on her mother's face, nor the dismay in Ross's dark eyes, the clenching of his hand. There was a moment's silence as she left the room, then Ross bent forward.

'Mrs Sinclair,' he said urgently, 'Bridget is all right with me. You could never think that I would do anything to hurt Bridget.' There was an obvious distress on his face.

Morag reddened still more. A direct approach like this embarrassed her. 'I should hope not,' she said frostily.

David frowned. 'Of course we know that, Ross,' he said quickly.

Morag flashed him a look. How could they know any such thing. But, 'Perhaps you have a young sister of your own, Mr Ledoux?' she asked brightly.

'No. I am the only one,' Ross answered quietly. But the first shadow had come over his happiness. For now he knew the why of that formal approach, remembered other small things. Bridget's mother did not approve of him as a husband for her daughter. And Bridget was very close to her family.

But Bridget was returning, smiling at him as she sat down beside him again. It was for Bridget as it was for him. What they had found together was real. He knew it. So — it was up to him.

7

Doctor Murray steered his car round the bend to take the rising road beyond the post office, pulling out slightly as he did so to avoid a young couple who were coming, hand in hand, down the road towards him. He glanced at them, recognizing the man by his height and — he braked quickly, pulling into the side of the road when he had passed them.

'Hello there, Bridget,' he called, but Bridget still with her hand in Ross's was coming back to the car, smiling cheerfully.

'Hello, Uncle Alan. Have you had a good holiday?'

'Evening, Ledoux.' The doctor smiled at Ross. 'Yes, we had a very good time.' He looked at Bridget critically. 'Bridget my dear, you look blooming. From all those reports I had of you I expected to see a pale little shadow. How are you feeling?'

'Very well again. I've even had to take out the little pleats I had to put in my skirts.'

The doctor laughed. 'That's a good sign. Well, I'm very pleased to see you looking so well, Bridget.' He looked at Ross. 'Things all right with you, Ledoux?'

'Everything is going fine, doctor,' Ross answered. 'Did Paris come up to expectations?'

'It certainly did. Aunt Janet had a marvellous time among those shops, Bridget. She enjoyed the last few days with Catriona and the baby too.'

'Was Hugh not there?'

'Just the first day. Then he went out on an exercise.' He looked from one to the other, 'Where are you two off to now?'

'Just for a walk,' it was Ross who answered. 'A short one.'

Bridget flashed him a look of affection. 'Ross won't let me walk too far, Uncle Alan. He's very strict with me.'

'Just as well.' The doctor was amused. 'Well, how about coming along later, Bridget, say about eight o'clock, and I'll give you a check over. Perhaps your father or mother would run you along.'

'I'll get my car and bring Bridget along, doctor,' Ross said.

'Good. See you then, Bridget.' Alan Murray started his engine again.

'Is he really your uncle?' Ross asked as Bridget and he walked on again. 'I haven't quite got the relationship. I mean is he your mother's brother, or is Mrs Murray your father's sister?'

'Neither,' Bridget answered. 'It's just we've always known them and I suppose now we are almost related. Oh, you didn't know that Catriona was married to Hugh. He's the Murray's son.'

'I see,' Ross said slowly. 'And is Hugh a doctor too?'

'Yes. In the Navy. I think Catriona

194

and he grew up together — they're the same age. As far as I can remember they were always together.'

'And your other sister? Didn't your father say something about her husband being a relation?'

'Oh, he's a second or third cousin or something. We didn't really know him until he came as a temporary minister in Inverness at the beginning of last year. Then he came out to visit us.'

'And married your sister.'

Bridget smiled. 'Catriona and I both think Sheena married him. She's bossy.'

'Is he younger than she is?'

'Oh, no, they're both twenty-five.'

'I see,' Ross said again. He released Bridget's hand and stepped behind her as a car came towards them. It passed and he came to her side again. 'All nice and tidy,' he said quietly. 'It's a pity that the Murrays hadn't another son and he would have done for you.'

Bridget looked at him quickly for there had been an underlying bitterness in his quiet tone which she had never heard before. She flushed. So Ross had noticed what she had hoped he had not marked. She put her hand in his again, gripping tightly. 'Do you think I would have wanted him, Ross?'

Ross gave her a shamed look. 'No,' he said. 'No. You want me.'

'Of course.' Bridget looked up at him, giving him her love, and he knew it, with every look, every small touch.

He took his hand away and put his arm round her as they turned from the main road on to a track which led by a small burn. 'Maybe I'm wondering, belatedly, why that should be,' he said. 'For after all — ' he smiled at her lovingly. But Bridget knew, sadly, it was not just that.

Behind them the doctor's car had gone on past the manse and the hotel and so to his own house which stood on the hillside above the row of fishermen's cottages on the north shore of the bay. Janet Murray had his meal ready for him, and while he washed his hands she was dishing up, so that it was not until they sat down at the table that she asked him if he had any other calls for that evening.

'I hope not,' she went on. 'That's plenty for a first day after a holiday. No doubt as soon as they discover you're back they'll all be trodding a path to the door.'

'I don't doubt it,' her husband agreed. 'I've just got young Bridget coming in about eight. I met her on the road and told her to come along, so that I can give her a check.'

'Bridget? Oh, how is the poor child? Still looking a wraith of herself?'

'She's looking remarkably well, Janet. Eyes bright. A good colour.' He smiled. 'Nothing like what I expected.'

'I am glad. Morag always said she'd get well quickly in her own home, with Achinlaig's good air.'

The doctor's eyes twinkled. 'I think Bridget has had something else apart from air and home cooking to forward her recovery.'

'Yes. You always said she had a strong

constitution. You'd better finish this off, Alan.' She took his plate off him to refill it.'

The doctor watched her. 'Thank you,' he began eating again. 'You know that Canadian who is working for the Forestry people, Janet? He came a month or so before we went away?'

'Yes, of course,' Janet said. 'He's so big he could never go unnoticed. Ledoux, isn't it? I don't think I ever heard any more.'

'Bridget calls him Ross,' Alan Murray said mildly.

'Bridget?' Janet stared. 'Bridget?' Her eyes widened with amusement. 'No?'

The doctor laughed and nodded. 'Yes. I met them walking along the road, hand in hand.'

'Well! I'd never have thought it. So that's what she meant!' she exclaimed.

'What? Who?'

'Morag. I had a word with her on the phone. She said something dreadful was happening and she didn't know what to do about it. She's coming along in the morning to see what I think. Of course she couldn't tell me over the phone or else Phemie would have been joining in with her advice. I've been wondering ever since what on earth it could be, but now I know. Bridget!'

'Why not? Nothing wrong with the fellow is there?'

'Oh, you know Morag.'

'Well, she should be pleased Bridget is having a love affair. I'll say it was certainly aiding her recovery. Mind you,' he smiled again, 'he does look at her as if she was something very precious, wrapped up in cotton wool as it were.'

'Morag will certainly not approve of Ledoux for Bridget. Not that she would approve of anyone for Bridget. Catriona thinks Bridget is destined to be the family prop, the one who stays at home to look after the old folk.'

'Why Bridget?'

'Because she's the youngest one, I suppose.'

'She isn't the youngest. There's Dave.'

'But Dave is a boy.'

The doctor snorted. 'What nonsense! These are the nineteen-seventies, not the eighteen-seventies. Besides, I'd have thought Sheena would have been the chosen one for that. She's more like her mother.'

'She's too like her mother. Sheena likes all her own way too. Now Bridget has always been the quiet docile one.'

'Well, I've always thought our little Bridget had quite a bit of steel beneath that shy exterior of hers. Come to think of it she wasn't a bit shy tonight, even though I met her with her young man. Of course neither her mother nor her sisters were there, Sheena in particular.'

'Yes, Sheena was always overpowering. Well, I'm glad Bridget is having some fun. I must have a word with her when she comes tonight.' She laughed and shook her head. 'I'd never have thought of that, I'm looking forward to seeing those two together.'

But Janet was not to see them together until the Sunday. While Bridget came in to see the doctor Ross sat outside in his car and though Mrs Murray had a word with Bridget when she came out, all she saw of Ross was when he got out of his car when Bridget went to join him. On the Sunday after church she had paused to say a few words to David when she saw Bridget going quickly past her to join Ledoux waiting for her at the gate. She smiled as she saw them go off down the road, and as she walked on down the path heard Morag's sharp 'You see?' in her ear.

'How pretty Bridget looks in that outfit,' Janet murmured. But Alan was just behind her too and as they reached the gate he was telling Mrs Sinclair how pleased he was with Bridget.

'She's going on fine,' he continued. 'I was afraid she might be feeling a bit down after what she's been through but — ' there was a gleam of mischief in his eyes as he looked at Morag, 'nothing like a bit of admiration for boosting the morale.'

Morag gave him a pained look, but

there were other people waiting to claim her attention. Janet called, 'I hope you enjoy your dinner tonight, Morag,' as she moved away with her husband and got in return a slight lift of Mrs Sinclair's eyebrows.

But truth to tell Morag was quite looking forward to the dinner at the hotel. After all the young man no doubt thought he should repay her hospitality, she told herself, having quite forgotten that the invitation from Ross had come before her own invitation. She had been to the hairdressers on Friday and intended to grace the occasion by wearing one of her most becoming dresses. Late August was a busy time at the hotel and though most of the guests there would be strangers, there might happen to be someone who would know who she was. In any event Mrs Robertson, if she had heard that Mr Ledoux was having guests for dinner would be sure to want to see who those guests were. That, of course, was what had troubled her when Ledoux had first issued his invitation.

Now she had decided that it would be as well if someone was to see Ledoux in the company of the minister and herself as well as of Bridget. In the past David had taken under his wing, as it were, people who had been staying temporarily in Achinlaig, people whom Morag herself might not have accepted as friends, but to whom she was always ready to be gracious. What more likely than that they had done the same in this case, and that Ledoux, in gratitude would be prepared to take Bridget on any little trips he might have to make. That, at any rate, was what she intended the village to think, and she had almost persuaded herself that that was the way it was. Bridget, of course, was being a little perverse, even imagining herself falling in love. But soon and with the help of a judicious word here and there Bridget would come down from the clouds and see how it really was.

Bridget herself, now that she knew

that Ross had guessed something of her mother's dislike of him, was viewing the coming evening with mixed feelings. She wanted to spend the evening with Ross, but would have preferred to spend it alone with him. But she knew what he was doing and loved him for it. And there was still time for her mother to change her mind — she had never seemed to dislike or resent either Hugh or Tom. Why — and how could she dislike Ross? Her father, at any rate, did like him. She was sure of that.

The minister was looking forward to the evening without reservations. He smiled affectionately at his wife and daughter as they came to join him in the hall, telling them they would both outshine any glamorous guests there might be at the hotel. Morag smiled as she led the way from the house and Bridget, following and getting into the back of the car — for they were not to walk the half mile from the manse to the hotel — was telling herself that tonight everything was going to be all right.

As the car turned into the hotel courtyard she saw Ross standing at the top of the steps leading to the entrance. He came quickly down to them as Morag turned the car into a nearby parking space, and if there was now a wariness in his manner which had never been there before he masked it well as he greeted them. He held the door for Mrs Sinclair to get out and then, for he had no intention of dissembling, of pretending, opened the rear door and lifted Bridget out as he alway did, keeping hold of her hand as they went up the steps and into the hotel.

As they were taken to a table in the lounge, as a comfortable chair was pulled forward for her, and their coats were taken from them, Morag could find nothing to fault the young man. She said she would like a sherry and when their drinks came sat back and proceeded to enjoy herself. When they went into the dining room they had been given a table in the window from which she had a view of the whole room, there was a bowl of low flowers in the centre of the table which none of the other tables seemed to boast, dinner when it came was good. David was obviously enjoying himself and Morag was her most charming self. Bridget began to relax too, and if she did not talk so much or so naturally to Ross as she did when she was alone with him, the minister at least noticed that his daughter was not so shy as she had been, not so ready to wait for her mother to answer any questions, much more ready to express her own opinions. He was pleased and — he looked at the young man seated opposite him — he was glad she had Ross. For that she had Ross, unlike his wife, he did not question for one moment.

Dinner over they went back into the lounge to have their coffee. 'I think that table in the corner,' Ross suggested. He smiled at Bridget. 'Bridget, if you would like to take your mother up to my room you may do so. If you want to powder your nose?'

Bridget's eyes twinkled. 'Is it shining?'

'Sure.' Ross grinned as he put up his hand and touched the tip of her nose with one finger. He put his hand in his pocket and brought out a key, holding it to her. 'First floor, on the right,' he said. 'Mrs Sinclair? Would you like to go upstairs?'

Morag's eyebrows had lifted slightly. But 'Yes, I would,' she said.

'I'll order coffee while you're away,' Ross said easily. 'Would you like anything to drink with it?' Then as Mrs Sinclair said a sedate, 'No thank you,' turned to the minister. 'How about you, Mr Sinclair?'

But Bridget was leading the way to the stairs and her mother followed her. She opened her mouth to say something, hesitated, changed her mind and, instead, remarked casually that she had seen Mrs Robertson in the background at the reception desk. 'I've no doubt she knew who Mr Ledoux was having as his guests tonight.'

'I expect so,' Bridget said quietly. 'Are you enjoying it, Mother?' she asked hopefully.

'It was a very nice meal,' Morag admitted. 'Your father seemed to enjoy it. And now, I've no doubt, he's indulging himself in a whisky.'

Bridget laughed. 'Why not?' They had reached the top of the stairs and turned to the right. She was looking at the numbers on the doors. 'This one,' she said and opened the door with the key, leaning forward to switch on the light and then letting her mother go before her.

Morag looked about her critically. The room — it was a decent size for a single room — was tidy at least. There were several things on the dressing table a row of shoes and boots against one wall, a pile of books on a table near the window, but that was all. There was another door and she opened it. 'Oh, he has his own bathroom has he.'

Bridget smiled as she moved to the dressing table, renewing her lipstick, combing her hair, looking at Ross's small possessions with a soft light in her eyes.

Her mother came back. 'It must be costing quite a bit to stay here for so long, mind you. I suppose the Forestry people will be paying the bill.'

'I wouldn't know,' Bridget's tone for once was a trifle dry. 'But if they are it must be because Ross is worth it to them.'

'Oh, I've no doubt Mr Ledoux is good at his job,' Morag said lightly.

Bridget took a deep breath. She was going to ask her mother to call him Ross. She was going to ask her now. 'Mother,' she began.

But Morag was not listening. She was turning before the mirror. 'Am I all right at the back, Bridget? Good. We'd better get down again.'

Bridget stood to one side to let her go before her. Perhaps this was not a good moment. But tomorrow, in the morning when they were alone together, she would ask her.

Downstairs the coffee was already on the table and the minister was contentedly sipping his whisky. Ross stood up, pulled out a chair for Mrs Sinclair, and turned the coffee tray towards Bridget. Again Morag's eyebrows lifted slightly and she gave her daughter a look of amusement but Bridget, having no thought on this occasion of deferring to her mother, did not even see as she lifted the coffee pot.

'When do you return to Canada, Mr Ledoux?' Morag asked as she received her coffee cup. 'I expect you'll be anxious to get back to your own country.'

Ross looked at her straightly. 'I've found my time over here most rewarding,' he said quietly. 'My year will be up at the beginning of November.'

Over two months yet, Morag thought Was he to be here all that time?

'You'll be remaining in Achinlaig till then, Ross?' the minister asked.

'Yes.' Ross hesitated and glanced at Bridget. 'There are suggestions that my tour of duty be extended by six months. So — ' he went on deliberately, 'as our winters in Canada can be severe for anyone not used to them, I'm looking carefully into it.'

David's eyes twinkled. He glanced at his wife, but Mrs Sinclair either had not heard or did not want to hear. She was looking to the doorway, giving one of her best and most graceful bows. She had been disappointed that there had been no one in the dining room or the lounges whom she knew, but here at last was someone. 'There's Ian Watson just come in,' she said brightly.

'Is it?' Bridget followed her gaze. There was colour in her cheeks for she had heard what Ross had said.

But Ian, after hesitating in the doorway, was coming towards them. 'Hello, Mrs Sinclair.' He nodded to the others. 'Having a night off too, are you. How are you now, Bridget?'

'Very well, thank you,' Bridget answered.

'I saw your father at church this morning, Ian,' the minister said. 'He was telling me about all the alterations you're having done. I'll be over to have a look at them.'

'Yes, you'll see a change.'

Ross had given Mrs Sinclair a quick look. Was that it? Was he interfering in some plans she had for Bridget? He stood up and moved his chair. 'Care to join us, Watson?' he said easily. 'What can I get you to drink?'

'Nothing, thanks all the same, old man,' Ian said cheerfully. 'I'm supposed to be meeting two fellows.' He glanced to the door. 'Ah, here they are. Be seeing you all,' he looked around them. 'Bridget, you grow prettier every time I see you,' he went on audaciously. He grinned, 'Better watch it, Ledoux, or I'll cut you out.' He put up a hand and went off.

The minister laughed and Bridget, though her colour was even brighter returned Ross's amused lift of his eyebrows with a laughing glance. But

Morag was frowning. That had not been a good idea. 'He's a foolish young man, Ian Watson,' she said severely.

'Oh just young and a bit brash,' David said indulgently. 'You'll know the Watson farm, Ross? They've been having all their farm buildings rebuilt, Ian's father was telling me. Other improvements too.' He went on telling Ross in detail, while Ross listened attentively, putting in a polite word here and there.

Bridget was leaning back in her seat, drinking her coffee, listening too. Morag, too, seemed to be listening, but she was studying her host. There was nothing flamboyant in his dress tonight, she had to admit that. Nor could she fault him in his behaviour or his manners. Apparently he knew how to behave in company such as this. He had been very attentive to both herself and to David, and if he had been too attentive to Bridget to her way of thinking, well — She looked at him pensively. He had not joined David in his whisky, she noticed. No doubt he preferred his beer. Was he a hard drinker? That she could well imagine. She marked again the scar on his face and remembered what she had first thought of that. Probably she had been right. Tonight he was quiet and well-behaved, but in other company he would no doubt be both rough and loud. He was so dark, so huge and — her gaze went to where he was resting one of his hands on the arm of his chair — those big hands! Clean, of course, with well-kept nails, but hard and work-worn, and her daughter — she gave a little delicate shudder — allowed him to touch her with those hands.

She did not realize that both the young people opposite to her were watching her. Ross, conscious of her scrutiny had glanced at her several times as he listened to the minister and now he caught that stare at his hand, that shudder. He reddened, his head bent, he moved his hand quickly from chair arm to his knee. So it was not another more eligible suitor, but himself. He was back to where he had been on Thursday. And not only was it a suspicion of his morals, but an aversion to his appearance. That, of course, had never even occurred to him. But — he glanced sombrely, even a little wistfully at Bridget, no doubt beside Bridget, who was small and fragile and beautiful, he seemed clumsy, ungainly.

But Bridget too had seen both her mother's look and Ross's reaction. Her face flamed, her chin lifted and in that moment though she did not know it, she left behind her unquestioning girlhood, her acceptance that her mother knew best, that whatever she did or thought was right. 'More coffee, Mother?' she asked. She leaned over Ross and deliberately laid her hand over his where it rested on his knees as she reached for her mother's cup.

Mrs Sinclair, who had no idea that her critical observation had been observed in turn, and who was far from crediting Ross Ledoux with any sensitivity at all, looked startled and gave Bridget one of her half-smiling, pointed looks, which had been so effective with her girls in the past when they had been doing something of which she did not approve. But this time Bridget merely gave her a cool look. 'Something not right, Mother?' she questioned. 'Have I put too much milk in your coffee?'

It was Morag's turn to colour slightly. 'No no, dear. It's very nice. Make it the same again.'

Bridget took the cup and slowly lifted her hand, concentrating again on pouring her coffee. The little by-play had not been lost on Ross. He looked lovingly at Bridget, but the last thing he wanted was to make a breach between her and her mother. He had hoped — and he did not know where he had gone wrong — that everything was going to be perfect for Bridget.

'I think we could do with some more coffee, Bridget,' he said quietly. 'How about it? Shall I order some?'

'Yes,' Bridget agreed and smiled at him.

'Right,' he looked around for a waiter. 'How about another drink, Mr Sinclair?'

David looked uncertainly at his empty glass. 'No, I'd better not. But — you tempt me, Ross.'

'Why not?' Ross smiled at him. With Bridget's father he could be completely at ease. And with her mother — he had to go on trying. 'What about you, Mrs Sinclair? Sure I can't persuade you to have anything?'

'No, thank you,' Morag smiled. 'I'm enjoying the coffee.' She looked at David indulgently. 'I'm sure you can let yourself be persuaded for once, David.'

A waiter came forward, Ross gave the order and turned back to the minister, 'You were telling me about that farm in Perthshire, Mr Sinclair.'

'Yes. In the Carse of Gowrie. Your uncle's farm, Morag. Now that is fine fertile land.'

They went on talking, the brief moment of tension marked only by Bridget and Ross, had passed. An hour later when they rose to go Morag, being helped into her coat, said graciously that she had enjoyed her evening very much, and was surprised to know that she meant it.

'And so have I,' the minister said heartily. 'Thank you very much, Ross. A delightful evening.'

Ross looked down at Bridget as he held her coat for her. 'Shall I walk you home, Bridget?' he asked quietly.

'Yes,' Bridget smiled. 'I'm sure it'll be a fine night.'

Mrs Sinclair gave them a surprised look. 'We have the car, Bridget. Did you forget?'

David laughed. 'Come along, Morag,' he said cheerfully. 'They want a walk.'

Morag's smile became a little fixed. It was too bad of David. But she allowed herself to be taken out to the car, she started her engine and backed out as Ross guided her round, and her mouth tightened as she saw Bridget put her hand into Ledoux's arm as the car moved away.

'It seems silly to walk on a dark night when we have the car,' she said tartly. 'I'm surprised at you encouraging her, David.'

'Oh, Morag,' the minister shook his head at her. 'We aren't so old, you and I, that we've forgotten. And I'm sure we've had a very nice evening.'

'Very pleasant,' Morag agreed.

'He's a nice young man. I enjoy talking to him.'

'And I'm sure he enjoys talking to you, David.' Morag brightened. Probably Ledoux was a little lonely so far from his own home and was glad to be accepted by the minister and his family. That was the way it was. If she could keep it on the right footing and prevent Bridget being foolish everything would be all right.

The minister yawned as they entered the house. 'I'm for bed,' he said. 'No need to wait for Bridget, Morag. She'll have her key.'

'I'll wait,' Morag said sedately. 'She can't be very long.'

David smiled to himself as he went up the stairs but Morag did not have very long to wait before she heard her daughter's key in the door. She smiled as she came into the room. 'Your father is away off to bed. He seems to have enjoyed his evening. I did too.'

'Did you, Mother?' Bridget's tone was cool. She took a deep breath and gave her mother a straight look. 'Mother, why don't you like Ross?'

'Mr Ledoux?'

'Ross,' Bridget said firmly. 'Why don't you like him?'

'Bridget!' Mrs Sinclair looked pained. 'I don't dislike Mr Ledoux, dear. I'm sure he's a most estimable young man. Why should you think that I dislike him?'

'You look at him as if you did,' Bridget's voice faltered. 'You don't even call him by his Christian name.'

Morag's eyes opened wide. 'Bridget, my dear, with your father's calling I have to meet many people, quite nice people I must admit like Mr Ledoux, who come and go. But I can't be expected to admit them all to the degree of intimacy you suggest. As for the way I look at him I don't know what you mean. Unless,' she smiled, 'you expect me to look at him the way you do. There, Bridget, I'm sorry, but I must speak seriously to you. I didn't mean to. We know you've been ill, you're not yourself yet. But — dear,' she went on gently and had now convinced herself that she was speaking to Bridget entirely for her own good, 'aren't you reading too much into it, imagining something which isn't there?'

'Am I?' Bridget though her hands were gripping tightly, went on firmly, 'I know that I'm not. Mother, it isn't the way you think — '

'Bridget!' Morag interrupted. She sighed. 'What do you know of men. Of men of the world like Mr Ledoux, who is, after all, so much older than you. You'll embarrass him, dear, if you try to read anything more into his kind actions of taking you about while you are convalescing, and he is at a loose end. And — you'll have everyone talking about you.'

Bridget's face flamed and then whitened. 'Mother,' she began but Morag had put a hand up wearily to her head.

'Bridget please, don't let us have any more arguments. We've had a pleasant evening. Don't spoil it. You're making my head ache.'

For a moment Bridget stared at her mother. Then, 'Goodnight, Mother,' she said quietly and turned away, going quickly up the stairs to her own room. She shut the door behind her but did not switch on her light. She groped her way to her window and looked out. She wished she could see their star but she could not. They had looked at it on their way down. And — her mother was wrong. Ross did love her, as she did him. She thought of those few minutes they had had together — she knew it was not the way her mother said.

8

For Bridget, of course, there were a few
doubts, a few fears, during the next
few days. Was she, because she was
inexperienced — and she knew she was
that — therefore unable to read, to
understand the man she loved? For
Ross, too, there were fears. Would
Bridget, with that gentleness which was
so much a part of the girl he loved, be
influenced by her mother, begin to
wonder if she could give him more than
she was giving now, begin to draw
back?

But once they were together those
fears were soon dispelled. For both
knew that what they had found together
was real and deep, that their growing
love and understanding could not be
marred by anyone's disapproval, even if
that disapproval could cast a shadow
over their happiness. Doggedly Ross

kept to the course he had set himself. For though the weeks since she had come home to Achinlaig had shown a great change in Bridget, she still had a fragility about her, she had still not got back her complete strength. If she had been alone in the world he would have wanted to marry her immediately, to give him the right to take care of her. But she was not alone, so she had to have the full period of convalescence, and during that time he had to show her parents even if they, or her mother, could not like him, that he was to be trusted to take care of her in the future. For he did intend to take her to Canada, which, no doubt, to them seemed far away.

Bridget made no further attempt to get her mother to change her attitude to Ross. She was hurt by it, but she did not let it influence her in any way. Wherever they were going she mentioned it quite calmly and casually, but she no longer tried to share her joy with her mother.

Mrs Sinclair, with a capacity for not seeing things she did not want to see told herself that Bridget was heeding her words, that before long the young man would go away and be forgotten, and if anyone in the village said anything to her about Bridget and marriage, she gave them one of her pained and cool smiles at the absurdity of any such idea. She did not realize that by her attitude in refusing to accept the fact that her daughter was being honourably courted by Ross Ledoux, she started the very gossip she wanted to avoid.

For soon everyone was taking sides. There were those who said cheerfully why should Bridget not have fun, that the young people were obviously in love. There were others who shook their heads solemnly, said poor Mrs Sinclair was rightly worried, that she was afraid of what might happen, for Bridget was an innocent child, the young man — well, everyone knew now what did happen even to a girl like the minister's daughter.

Bridget, who knew the value of all that was being said, who knew the truth, took it all serenely and with some amusement. But it distressed Ross. To have Bridget looked at, talked of in that fashion — Why, having made and still making his intentions as clear as he could it had happened he could not understand. He had not yet realized that much as he wanted to, try as he did, he could never protect Bridget from everything unpleasant in life.

But August had given place to September and they were spending all their free time together and nothing, neither gossip nor disapproval, could spoil their joy, their happiness in being together. They saw each other every day, even if it was just for a short time. When Ross was putting in an extra long day at his work, Bridget would walk along to meet him as he finished. She had been taken to the camp, had met the older man who was his assistant, the group of younger men who formed his team; she had been shown just what they were doing and realized again the pride, the interest Ross had in his work. When he had to go to Inverness Bridget went with him, and at the weekends they explored the countryside together, going often to look at the marvellous colourings of the sea at Gruinard Bay, taking the fine new road which opened out the magnificence of Torridon; going out for a meal together on Saturday and Sunday evenings.

Wherever they were going Ross always called at the manse for Bridget and made a point of going in with her when they got back. Sometimes he would stay for a drink of coffee, on occasions he was asked for tea on a Saturday or a Sunday. For Morag, too, was keeping to her role of gracious hostess, apart from the fact that she knew what her husband expected of her. The minister liked the young man more and more, was pleased to see Bridget so happy and though he was a little troubled by his wife's manner he was sure she would come round eventually. One day when he was alone with Ross he had asked him about his religion and had been told readily what Ross had already told Bridget.

Morag had been aghast when David told her. 'You didn't ask him, David? Why — he'd take it as an impertinence. Didn't he?' she went on hopefully. For if that were so they might see less of him.

'Nonsense,' David said. 'He was very ready to talk to me. And very honest.'

Ross had been pleased to answer the minister, was ready to answer any other questions Bridget's father cared to ask him. For did it not show that at last he was being accepted. Perhaps after that he relaxed a little of his wariness when he was at the manse, for a few days later when he was there for tea, when Bridget had risen and started to clear the table he had got up too, carrying the dishes to the kitchen for her, picking up a towel when he got there to dry them for her as she washed them.

They had not got very far. Morag, who had been called to the telephone, came in at that and raised astonished eyebrows.

'Thank you, Mr Ledoux,' she said brightly, 'but I've never yet expected my guests to do the chores. Bridget, what are you thinking of?' She held her hand out for the towel. 'Maybe you'll join Mr Sinclair in the living room.'

Ross, some colour in his dark face, had done so. He had better not try that again. For he was still Mr Ledoux, still a guest and not one of the family. Bridget had bitten her lip but said nothing. For by now she knew that it was not just Ross himself, it would not have mattered who the young man was.

When the Frasers had returned from their holiday Alec Fraser had asked her if she would like to come and work part time with him at the bank after her two months was up. Bridget had accepted with alacrity. Ross was to be in Achinlaig till the end of October and in that way she could stay in Achinlaig for that month too without being entirely dependent on her family. To return to Edinburgh for a full time job for what she knew would be only one month seemed pointless. So here was the solution. She told Alec she would be glad to help him on a temporary basis.

To Bridget's surprise Mrs Sinclair welcomed the idea with enthusiasm. She was not left long in doubt as to why that should be.

'As a matter of fact, Bridget,' Morag went on, 'Mary and I discussed it some time ago. And, of course, Alec thought it was an excellent suggestion. You know how difficult he finds it to get any help here.'

'Yes,' Bridget eyed her mother warily. 'It is just on a temporary basis, of course,' she said firmly.

'Oh, but dear, there is no need for you to go away again. We love having you at home, your father and I. And you are such a help to me. So just forget about it being temporary.' Morag smiled brightly. 'This last year I've been feeling I'd too much to do. But with you here — I'm planning to go down to Glasgow to spend a few days with Sheena now you are here to stay with your father. And when Catriona has her next baby I'll be able to go down to be with her with an easy mind.'

Bridget stared. 'I didn't know Catriona was having another baby.'

'Oh, not yet, Bridget.' Mrs Sinclair gave a little laugh. 'But they do want to have another child, so — '

Bridget gave her mother a straight look and changed the subject. So that was it. She should have guessed, of course, for there had been other revealing remarks. She remembered now her mother saying to one friend how delightful it was to have Bridget at home to help her, saying to another how she did not know now what she would do without Bridget to do all the little time-consuming things.

But September too was moving on quickly and in the week before Bridget's birthday when they went into

Inverness, Ross drove Bridget to the hospital so that she could have a chest X-ray. Dr Murray was very satisfied with her, but he wanted the information so that, he told them, he could give her a final check the next week. While they were in Inverness, too, Ross was given some confidential information from his superiors. Threats of damage and destruction against the forests had been received from some dissident group and everyone had to be on the alert for any prowlers who looked as if they might cause trouble.

'They think they'll likely go, if at all, for one of the larger, well-grown forests,' Ross told Bridget. 'But we'll all have to keep our eyes open. After these dry, hot days we've had this month, everything is like tinder. Probably merely a threat to cause a nuisance, of course,' he added cheerfully.

But nevertheless when Saturday came he drove to the camp when they went out in the afternoon, leaving Bridget sitting in the car at the end of the track while he went off to make a check. He was back in a few minutes, saying everything was O.K.

'I guess if there had been any strangers in or around Achinlaig we'd have heard of it by now,' he said dryly.

Bridget smiled. 'I don't doubt it,' she agreed.

Ross started his car and they moved off, taking a side road which would take them round the southern arm of the bay. As their afternoon had been shortened they were not planning to go very far but were just making for a stretch of coast which was usually deserted, where the Atlantic pounded on a wide strip of sand and from where Ross liked to bathe. A few miles of narrow, twisting road brought them to the place where they left the car off the road, and started to pick their way over the dunes to the shore. It was a fine clear day and very warm for late September. There was no sound but the pounding of the waves, and the air was lovely.

Bridget took some deep breaths. 'It's a grand day for a bathe.' She looked archly at Ross. 'I wonder how long it'll be before I'm allowed to bathe?'

Ross grinned down at her and squeezed the hand he held. 'Maybe by next summer. If we can find you a lake which is not too cold.'

They were out of sight of both car and road and the fine stretch of pale sand was completely deserted. Ross looked about him. 'How about here, Bridget?'

'Fine.' Bridget settled herself on the rug he spread for her, leaning back to enjoy the sun on her face as Ross strode away. He came back in his bathing trunks, dropping his clothes in a heap beside her. Bridget smiled at him and watched his tall and taut figure with a possessive and sensual pride as he strode away, feeling an exquisite shiver of delight go through her just at the sight of him. She smiled to herself as she saw him wade into the water, meeting the high waves, swimming strongly. She loved him and — she closed her eyes a little against the sun but still watching him — not long now before they would be completely together.

When she saw him coming out of the water she reached for the towel, and had it ready to hand to him when he reached her. He took it, towelling himself vigorously as he stood smiling down at her.

'I expect it was cold,' she said.

'Like ice. Exhilarating. Freshened me up.' Ross shook the water out of his thick hair and towelled it. 'Are you warm enough there, Bridget?'

'Oh, yes. That sun is really hot. It's a marvellous day for September.'

'Sure is.' He picked up his clothes and walked away, coming back in a few minutes to drop down beside her, stretching himself full length on his back, shutting his eyes. 'If you were to kiss me now you'd get a taste of salt,' he murmured.

Bridget's eyes twinkled. 'A salty kiss!

I haven't had one of those before. I must try one.' She bent over and kissed him, and he put an arm round her holding her gently.

'I love you,' he said softly. He opened his eyes and looked up at her. 'I'm not much good at words, sweetheart, am I? But — once we're married I'll do better.'

Bridget's smile was tender as she looked down at him. 'Are we getting married, Ross?'

'Of course! Aren't we? Isn't that the target?' Ross sat up quickly and then, seeing her expression lay back again contentedly. 'Tease! I think you've known that nearly as long as I have. And I've known — ' A smile softened his big, firm mouth. 'I won't say from the first day for I hardly saw you that day. I even had to stop for petrol I didn't need to see if I still had a passenger and what she was like.'

Bridget chuckled. 'Did you, Ross?'

'Sure.' He lay for a moment. 'Well, maybe that day too. But definitely at that dance, when I had to kiss you to see if you were going to be the little sister I'd always wanted when I was a kid or — ' his voice lowered and he caught her hand and held it against his cheek, 'my wife.' He took a deep breath. 'I don't know what I'd have done if you'd slapped my face or flounced away from me, sweetheart. But you didn't. You looked at me solemnly, as if you were looking for an answer.'

'Yes, I was,' Bridget agreed slowly. 'I didn't know what to think. And yet — I did know.'

'Yes. We both knew, my darling. Then,' he smiled again, 'next morning in church your father took as his text that bit about the man who found a pearl of great price, and I knew that was what I'd done, found my pearl of great price. Do you remember that sermon?'

Bridget shook her head, smiling ruefully. 'I don't think I heard one word of what father was saying. I was thinking about you, wondering when I would see you again, what your christian name was. I didn't know you were behind me.'

'No, I had the advantage of you. Not that we got very far that day. We managed about two words to each other before the crowd surged around. But the next night we met by chance, walked about a couple of hundred yards together, and in those few minutes settled our entire future.' His dark eyes twinkled at her and Bridget smiled happily.

'So we did. A pearl of great price,' she repeated slowly. 'Ross,' she went on, and there was a little catch in her throat, 'you won't think you have to keep your precious pearl in a silk-lined case, only to be looked at now and — '

She did not need to go on. Ross pulled her down to him. 'No,' he said. He kissed her with a fierce hunger. 'No! Bridget, we'll get married at the end of October, shall we. We won't need to wait any longer than that, will we?'

'No, Ross. I don't want to wait. Yes, the end of October.'

'I expect to have confirmation this week about the extra six months over here,' Ross went on, 'but, even so, I don't want to wait.'

'Nor I,' Bridget said again. 'Ross, you don't need to stay if you don't want to. I'll come to Canada with you then. Whenever you want to go.'

'I know, sweetheart. But, as I said, our winters can be hard. So we'll go over next spring and that will give you time to get acclimatized before the next winter. We're going to be stationed near Kyle, Bridget, so I'll be able to bring you over to Achinlaig for a day now and then. They want me to give a series of talks as, of course, there isn't so much outside work to do in the winter. And — there's a small furnished house we can have.'

'A house of our own,' Bridget said eagerly. 'Oh, I didn't expect that.'

'Very small, I believe,' Ross told her. 'With tiny rooms. So I don't know what you'll do with a big, clumsy husband in it.'

'You aren't clumsy,' Bridget said indignantly.

Ross smiled. 'Well, big certainly.'

'Of course,' Bridget said with satisfaction.

'You like the idea, sweetheart?'

'Oh, yes! It sounds wonderful, Ross. A little home of our own! I'll be able to cook for you.'

'Sure will. And we won't need to say goodnight under the tree beside the church.' He gave her a quick grin and then sobered. 'We'll tell your father and mother next Saturday, Bridget. On your birthday, and when your two months are up.'

'Yes,' Bridget murmured, but she was thinking now blissfully of sharing that home with Ross, of the happiness they would share. She slid down beside him, resting her head on his shoulder, putting her arm round him. Ross tightened his hold of her, rubbing his chin against her hair.

A few minutes later he sat up quickly, raising her with him. 'Someone is coming,' he said.

Bridget blinked and looked about her. The long stretch of sand was still deserted, there was no sound except the steady pounding of the waves. 'I didn't hear anything.'

Ross smiled slightly. 'I'm a woodsman. Remember?' He was looking to where a track curved round the dunes to where they had left their car. 'It may be someone who knows us, and I don't want them to get a wrong impression.' He gave her a quick grin, put up a hand to flatten his hair and then gave a little tug to her skirt. He caught her laughing look and his smile widened. 'I know, sweetheart. Half of them have got that impression already. Even your — ' He bit his lip and went on grimly, 'They're just waiting for me to seduce you and then be off and leave you. Why, I just don't know, but — It's Mrs Laurie, I think. Hasn't she some people staying with her?'

Bridget turned her head. 'Yes. Her brother and his wife and family. Ross,' she went on softly, 'I know. I always knew.'

'Yes.' Ross took a deep breath and looked at her.

But the group were coming nearer, the spell of the afternoon was broken. Mrs Laurie was calling to them cheerfully. She, they both knew, was not one who looked at them askance. 'Have you been bathing?' she went on.

'Ross has,' Bridget answered and gave him a fond look. 'He won't let me go in. Says it's too cold for me.'

'I expect it is,' Mrs Laurie agreed. 'The young ones wanted to see some real sand,' she said, pointing to the children scattering in front of them.

'Don't let them go into the water, Mrs Laurie,' Ross cautioned. 'They could get out of their depth in yards.'

'We won't,' Mrs Laurie promised and followed her friends.

Ross looked at his watch. He stood up, lifting Bridget. 'Time we made a move, sweetheart. By the time we go back for me to get changed — your mother won't like us to be late for tea.'

On the following Thursday Bridget went in the afternoon for Dr Murray to give her her final check. He already had the results of her X-ray, and after he had given her a thorough examination he sat down at his desk and smiled across at her.

'As I thought, Bridget,' he said. 'You're as sound as a bell. Not a trace of anything wrong with you. In fact, my dear, you're much fitter now than when you were home in the spring. I was a bit worried about you then. That, of course, was why you had that very nasty time. I'm sure you feel fit?'

'Oh, I do! Thank you for looking after me so well.'

'Thank you for being so good a patient. I haven't done much. That was you yourself — and your mother, of course. And,' he smiled, 'I think we must give a lot of the credit to someone else too, mustn't we?'

Bridget nodded, her eyes bright.

Alan Murray watched her a moment

with affection. Both he and Janet had always been very fond of Bridget. 'He's a big man, Bridget,' he said slowly. 'He's going to need a lot of loving.'

Bridget coloured a little, but her chin lifted and her look was straight. 'I will give him that, Uncle Alan — when the time comes.'

There was a flash of amusement in the doctor's eyes. 'No reason why you shouldn't, Bridget. No reason at all. But — you'll need to tell him that. For he's inclined to wrap you up in cotton wool as it were, isn't he?'

Bridget smiled tenderly. 'He does, doesn't he?'

'You tell him. As for your little rider, my dear, no need to tell me that. I can judge men.'

'A lot of other people can't,' Bridget said quietly.

'Well you know how people talk in our small community, Bridget. You don't let that worry you?'

Bridget shook her head. 'No. But it worries Ross.'

'Well he's older than you, Bridget. He's thinking of you. Got you on a bit of a pedestal, I'm afraid, my dear.'

'Yes,' Bridget smiled again. 'But — there's my mother too, Uncle Alan. And — she doesn't like Ross.'

The doctor did not pretend that he did not know what she meant. 'I wouldn't put it as high as that, Bridget. Morag — and I've known your mother longer than you have — likes everything to fit into her own preconceived pattern. And your Ross doesn't fit into any pattern, does he. She'll come round. In fact before long she'll have forgotten it wasn't her idea in the first place.'

'Maybe,' Bridget said slowly. 'But there's more to it than that, Uncle Alan.' Her clear eyes were troubled as she looked at him. 'Do you think if you're the youngest you have a duty to stay at home and look after your parents — I mean, when they are old?'

'I do not,' Alan said firmly. 'Besides,' he watched her shrewdly, 'you're not the youngest, Bridget. Yes, I know Dave is a boy, but you've as much right to your own life as he has, as Catriona and Sheena have. And,' he shook his head at her, 'your father and mother are still in their fifties. You don't think we're all settling down to real old age already, do you?'

Bridget smiled. Perhaps she had been imagining things. 'It does seem silly.'

The doctor got up and came round to her, patting her shoulder. 'Come along. Janet will have some tea ready for us. I think she's got a new coat she wants to show you.'

9

Bridget's birthday was on the Saturday and she woke early to see a fine crisp autumn day. For the first time there was a nip in the air, there were veils of gossamer on the bushes and a sky of clear blue. It was a lovely morning — of course it was bound to be a perfect day today. She was downstairs quickly, not that she could expect any post yet for Achinlaig did not get its mail until mid-afternoon, but there were her parents' presents to look at, another from the Murrays and a parcel from Mary Fraser. And — Ross was working this morning and though he had said nothing about calling on his way to the camp, she knew he would.

They were still at the breakfast table when she heard the familiar sound of his car stopping and jumped up, hurrying from the room to the hall.

David looked at his wife and laughed.

'A very important day this, I'm thinking, Morag,' he said.

Mrs Sinclair smiled. 'Oh, yes. What it is to be twenty-two.' That was not what David had meant and she knew it, for while she was dressing she had remembered something of which she had not thought for a long time. David had given her her ring on her birthday. But she, of course, had been twenty-four. She put the unwelcome thought to the back of her mind.

But Bridget had reached the front door and opened it as Ross was coming up the path. She pulled the door to behind her and laughed up at him. 'Why, Ross, I didn't know you were coming this morning.'

Ross opened his eyes wide. 'Did you not!' He put an arm round her, bending to kiss her. 'Many happy returns, my darling. So very many happy returns — all shared with me, of course.'

'Of course.'

He put a hand in his pocket and

brought out a flat parcel. 'I had to bring you your present.'

'Oh, thank you.' Bridget's eager fingers were busy with the wrappings, tearing the paper, taking out the flat jewellers' case, opening it. Her eyes sparkled as she saw the bracelet of linked amethysts, as she lifted it. 'Oh, how gorgeous! What a lovely present!'

Ross smiled as he watched her. 'They're the colour of your eyes when I kiss you.' He saw her eyes open wide and laughed as he corrected himself. 'After I kiss you.'

'Like now!' She kissed him. 'Thank you, darling. I thought my eyes were said to be dark blue like — ' She laughed up at him, thinking of that sapphire ring they had chosen together when last they were in Inverness. 'I didn't expect to get two presents today.'

'Two?' Ross tapped his inner pocket. 'That isn't a birthday present. You don't get that till after we've told your father and mother. Besides, you don't know anything about that.'

'Not a thing!' Bridget said gaily.

Ross kissed her again. 'Well, sweetheart, I'd be perfectly happy to stay with you all day like this, but I'd better get on. I'm going to go back after lunch, Bridget, just for a check. So after you get your post walk along and meet me, then we'll to to the hotel while I get changed before — ' he looked at her meaningly.

Bridget nodded. 'Yes, I'll do that.'

'But don't come any further than the car, sweetheart. Wait for me there if I haven't met you before that.' He gave her a quick grin, 'I shouldn't like to have to be told to go and wash my mouth out with soap today of all days.'

Bridget laughed at him, remembering that day when she had gone to meet him at the camp, recalling the unholy glee dawning on the face of the young man who had been at the receiving end of Ross's fluent tirade in a mixture of English and French, the consternation on Ross's face as he had swung round and seen her. She had backed quickly, telling him with an air of innocence when he came to her that he would have to give her some lessons in French, then sharing his rueful laughter. Now she laughed as she watched him going down the path, thinking as she always did how big and handsome he looked in his working garb, his trousers thrust into his high boots, his gaudy shirt. She waved to him as the car moved away and only then remembered that there would be no one at the camp this afternoon to receive any picturesque language. For she knew that all the young men were planning to go off to Inverness as soon as they finished at midday.

She paused in the hall. Did Ross think there really was danger? Had he heard anything else? But, of course, he was always ultra-cautious where she was concerned. And nothing would happen today! She went back into the dining room.

'That was Ross,' she said unnecessarily. 'Look at my lovely present.' She held it out for her mother's inspection. Today she had forgotten the shadow and was ready to share her joy. 'Isn't it beautiful?'

'It is indeed.' Morag might have reservations about the giver but could have none about the gift. And it was not a ring!

'A pretty thing.' David leaned over to look at it. 'What is it?'

'A bracelet of course.' Bridget tried it on, holding it this way and that. 'Look what a rich colour those stones are!' Did her eyes really turn to that lovely colour? She took it off, holding it to her mother again. 'I wonder when he got it. I didn't know he was getting this t — ' She checked quickly but no one had noticed. Morag was examining the bracelet and David was bending forward to look at it too.

'I suppose Ross is working this morning,' he said casually. 'Do we see him today, Bridget?'

'Oh, yes. This afternoon.' Bridget caught the amused speculation in her father's look and blushed vividly. She began hastily piling up the used dishes. 'I'll away and get washed up.' She went quickly from the room.

The minister smiled at his wife. 'As I thought, Morag.'

But for once Morag was not paying much heed. She was still looking at the bracelet. 'This is a costly thing, David. Do you — ' She wondered if it was right for Bridget to accept such a gift but obviously David had no such thought.

'I suppose it is,' he said lightly. 'The young man seems to have good taste.'

'Oh, aye. In this he has,' Morag admitted. And maybe it was by way of being a parting gift. She would hope so.

In the kitchen Bridget was smiling to herself. Almost she had given away their secret. For Ross must be there when they told them. He wanted it that way and so did she. They had all their plans made. They would go to the hotel, where she would wait while Ross changed from his working clothes. Then they would come back to the manse.

And in the evening when all was settled and she was wearing that lovely ring they would leave her father and mother to have their usual peaceful Saturday evening, and go to have a quiet dinner to themselves. But tomorrow night they intended to take not only her parents but the Murrays too to the hotel for a celebration dinner. She knew her father and mother had nothing special fixed for Sunday night and, tactfully she hoped, she had sounded Aunt Janet on Thursday so that the last minute invitations would, they were sure, be accepted. And as her father would marry them, Uncle Alan must be asked if he would give her away as he had done for both Catriona and Sheena. She smiled happily as she plunged her hands into the soapy water, looking out of the window at the garden. What a beautiful clear sky it was!

But by the time Bridget had got and opened her post and started off along the road towards the post office that afternoon much of the blueness of that sky had disappeared. The clouds were coming in from the west, the islands had disappeared, even the sea was grey. It almost seemed as if later they might have rain.

A car was coming towards her and she hesitated, but it was not their car and she went on, passing the post office and climbing the twisting hill away from the bay. Two or three other cars came down the road, but they all went quickly past her, and in minutes she had reached the top of the hill and turned the corner which brought in view the end of the track which led over a patch of cleared ground and into the forest. The car was there and she hurried on. For suddenly fear was gripping her; an unreasoning fear, for everything looked normal, the momentarily deserted road, the car in its usual position, the autumn afternoon serene and still. But Bridget was highland and she did not question that rising fear which was gripping her throat. She began to run, pausing for a fraction of a second as she reached the car, looking at it, remembering Ross's injunction for her to wait there for him, but knowing that this time she would not obey him. For Ross should have been here by now, he would not have lingered in the forest unless of necessity, today of all days.

In a moment she was out of sight of the road, with the trees all about her, running soundlessly on the grass-grown, rutted track. It was not far to the small cleared space which they called their camp, and where they kept the caravan in which they stored their tools, but before she even came in sight of it, she heard a crunching, the cracking of breaking twigs, the sounds of heavy footsteps. And through the lacework of the branches in front of her she could see movement, shadows, colour. She reached the opening and her wide, frightened eyes took in the scene. Ross was struggling with two men, appeared to be gripping with his left hand the wrists of a man with a ginger beard who was kicking him viciously, while with his right he returned the blows of another. For seemingly, even with the odds against him his height and his strength were telling, for at that moment a hard blow from his fist sent one assailant reeling backwards to fall heavily, and he turned his attention to the second man. But at that same moment Bridget pausing in the shadows of the trees, telling herself she must not hinder Ross by her presence, deciding how she could help him by rushing in if the man who had gone down made any movement, saw something which neither Ross nor his assailant could see. From the trees to the left of her another man was coming running, and he was holding what looked like a long piece of iron, he had it raised above his head.

Bridget's terrified warning scream of 'Ross! From your left!' rang out sharply.

Ross turned but, hampered as he was

by the man he was already overpowering, too late to avoid the vicious blow. It
came down on the front of his head
instead of the back, he fell forward to
his knees. Bridget made a frantic leap
forward, dropping down beside him,
clutching him, her horrified eyes seeing
that dreadful wound, the blood which
covered his face, his shirt, covered her
too.

But Ross was struggling for consciousness. 'Go, Bridget! For God's
sake go!' he muttered. 'Run.'

Bridget, on her knees, was cradling
him, wiping the blood from his eyes
with her hands, reaching to her pocket
for an ineffectual small square of
handkerchief, oblivious of danger. But
as she heard Ross's words, felt his
hands trying to raise her, push her
away, she looked round and saw,
without surprise, that the two men who
were on their feet were dragging the
man who had been down away among
the trees, heard in a moment the sound
of their crashing through the forest as

they made their hurried get-away.

'They've gone, darling, they've gone,' she whispered. She had got his larger handkerchief from his pocket now, was holding it over that gaping wound, but knew nothing she could do could staunch that bleeding. She could not move him, she knew that, for any moment he might lose consciousness altogether. Even her inexperienced eyes told her that. He might — She choked on the terrible thought. 'I'll have to go for help, Ross,' she whispered.

'Yes,' Ross tried hard to focus on her face, but somehow there was a haze over his dark eyes. 'Yes,' he muttered, 'Don't come back, Bridget. Don't.'

Bridget did not argue. 'Try to lie back,' she said, for if he lay flat perhaps the bleeding would cease. But Ross knew that once he fell back he would not rise again, and Bridget — Bridget was still here.

But Bridget had left him and was running frantically along the track back to the road. The fear which had brought her swiftly there was as nothing to the fear which was with her now. Terror was gripping her throat, showing in her eyes, for even in the few minutes which would take her to the road and back again Ross might die. She had no idea that her coat, her sweater, her skirt, her face and her hands were red with blood, no thought of the frightening sight she was as she rushed out on to the road, holding up her hands to stop a car which was only a few yards away and travelling towards Achinlaig.

But it did stop, its brakes were applied fiercely and it pulled into the side a few yards from her. There was a man and a woman in the front and momentarily, but only momentarily the woman shrank back. Quickly she wound down the window at her side as Bridget reached them.

'Please. Get help!' She was gasping as she tried to speak. 'The doctor. The police. Quickly.'

'An accident, Miss?' The man leaned forward. 'How? You're hurt?' He gave a swift look beyond her.

'Not me. It's Ross.' Bridget took a deep breath, trying for coherence. 'Mr Ledoux. At the forestry camp. He's been attacked. Three men.'

The woman leaned over to open the door to the rear. 'Get in. We'll take you,' she said.

Bridget shook her head. 'I must go back. He's badly injured.' The stark terror in her eyes told them what she dared not put into words. 'The post office. Half a mile on,' she went on. 'Quickly. Please!'

The man nodded, grasping the urgency. The woman slammed the door shut, the engine was restarted and as Bridget turned to run back along the track, she heard the car accelerating down the hill. From in front of her there was no sound. The attackers had not returned. As soon as she reached the clearing she saw that Ross had tried to move, that he had in fact pulled himself up so that there was a tree stump behind him. She dropped down beside him, saw with an overwhelming relief the slight flicker of recognition in his dull eyes, the movement of his hands.

'You shouldn't — ' he began, his speech so slurred that she could hardly hear, but she knew what he wanted to say.

'No, Ross, don't.' Her arms were round him. 'They've gone for help,' she told him but whether he heard or not she did not know for he was still trying to grasp her, to move her with a hand which had been at once so strong and so gentle when he touched her and was now so feeble. Bridget understood and humoured him, moving so that she was crouched behind him, shielded by his body. She was holding him against her, her cheek was against his, listening with a painful anxiety for any change in his laboured heavy breathing. There was no other sound in the forest now, no bird song, not even the buzz of an insect. How long would it be before they came? Not long surely, not long. For the car would have reached the post office almost by the time she had got back to Ross. Surely Doctor Murray would not be far away on a quiet Saturday afternoon. Sergeant MacPherson would be at home. Dear God, she prayed, let them come quickly, for even when they did come —

The minutes ticked by and Bridget as she crouched there, saw for the first time the heap of dry twigs a few yards from the caravan, the can of petrol standing beside it. They had been going to set fire to the forest and Ross, returning from his reconnoitre must have disturbed them. Supposing they came back — came back now to finish what they had started.

But there was still no sound in the silent forest and when the noise of approaching footsteps did come it was Ross, semi-conscious as he was who heard it first. He moved, trying to drag himself more upright. Bridget held him tightly.

'Don't move,' she said urgently. She

too listened. She heard the footsteps, the voices. They were coming along the track. 'It is help,' she whispered and the next instant a group of men emerged from the track to the clearing. Alan Murray was in front, beside him was the police sergeant; behind them a young constable and a middle-aged man whom Bridget did not realize was the driver of the car she had stopped.

The doctor dropped to his knees beside her. 'All right, Bridget,' he said quietly and put his arms out to move her gently. 'Let me.' He took her place in supporting Ross. 'She's all right now, Ross,' he said gently. 'Let go now, lad, let go.'

Ross seemed to stare at him for a moment, then his eyes closed and his head fell back. The doctor lowered him to the ground. Bridget gave a little whimper and her hands came out.

'No, no, Bridget,' Alan said quickly. 'He's just passed out. Better that way. Now let me see.' His capable hands were busy.

Sergeant MacPherson came to kneel beside Bridget. 'How did it happen, Bridget? Can you tell me?'

Bridget though she did not take her eyes from Ross for one moment told him baldly what she had seen, pointed to the heaped twigs and the petrol. The sergeant got up, went over and examined them, said something to the constable and the other man and came back as the doctor raised his head.

'I've got to have him to hospital immediately, sergeant. I suggest a helicopter. Get them to send one. Extreme urgency, tell them.'

The sergeant wasted no words. He nodded and strode away and Alan Murray looked at Bridget, saw that she knew and decided not to pretend to her. He gave her arm a brief pat and went on with his work. In minutes Sergeant MacPherson was back.

'On its way in minutes, doctor,' he said laconically.

'Good. It'll make all the difference.' Again he glanced at Bridget, sharing with her that brief glimmer of hope.

The sergeant looked at her too. 'Could you describe any of the men, Bridget?' he asked, and Bridget did her best for him. He wrote it down carefully while his constable was sent back to the cars, returning with an improvised stretcher. By then the doctor had done all he could for Ross, and he stood up. Bridget, her face white under the stains of blood, her eyes huge with fear, looked up at him wordlessly.

'He is a strong, healthy man,' Alan said quietly and put his hands out to help her to her feet as the other men came forward.

They lifted Ross carefully on to the stretcher and slowly carried him along the track to the open space beside the road. Here the helicopter was expected to come down, and in minutes they heard the whirring sound of its descending. Bridget, panic rising in her now, had only time to bend quickly to kiss Ross's bloodstained face, before he was being lifted as carefully into the machine. Her hands clasped tightly, her lips pressed closely together she stood watching as it rose again into the air.

The sergeant had gone to his car, was speaking again on his radio, for now they had a search on their hands. Dr Murray had a word with the stranger, and then put his arm round Bridget's shoulders, drawing her over to his car.

'I'll take you home now, Bridget,' he said. She had not cried yet and she should. Presently it would come. He let her sit in silence beside him as they travelled the short distance to the manse, and once there got out and put an arm about her again as they went up the path. He had hoped that David would be in his garden, but he was not, and Morag was alone in the living room as they entered.

She looked round, expecting to see Ledoux with Bridget and her usual, gracious smile froze and changed to horror. She let out a scream as she jumped up, coming to them, her hands outstretched. 'Bridget! What has happened?' She looked accusingly at Alan. 'What has he done to her? I knew this would happen! I knew it! What has he done?'

Bridget's deathly white face flamed, her young body stiffened. 'How dare you!' Her voice rose to a fury. 'How dare you! How — ' Then the tears came and she was crying brokenly, terribly.

The doctor pulled her into his arms. 'Bridget, Bridget! There, my dear.' He patted her head as she clung to him, burying her face on his shoulder, shaking now in her terrible grief.

Morag moved as if to take her from him. 'What has he done to her?' she asked again.

'Be quiet, Morag,' Alan said sternly. 'He has done nothing to her. Bridget isn't hurt. Just shocked. It is Ross — it is his blood.'

There was a quick step across the hall and David came in. 'Ross?' he questioned. 'What's happened?' He looked quickly from the weeping girl to his wife's shocked, indignant face. 'An accident with the car?'

'No. Ross has been attacked in the forest and,' the doctor looked meaningly at the other man, 'very badly injured. We've just had him taken to hospital by helicopter.'

Even Morag's expression changed at that for if she did not want Ross Ledoux in her family, considered him quite unsuitable for Bridget — and she had long ago convinced herself that Bridget's welfare was the sole reason for her disapproval — she did not want anything to happen to the young man. And if they had sent a helicopter to take the patient to hospital it must be very serious indeed.

The minister had recognized that too. He gave his wife a brief glance. 'And Bridget?' he asked quietly. 'Is she hurt too?'

'No,' Alan answered. 'She seems to have arrived just as it happened. Fortunately.' He looked down at Bridget, giving her another little pat. 'There,

Bridget,' he said again gently. 'I don't know what Ross will say to me if I let you make yourself ill again.' Bridget took a deep, shuddering breath and blinked hard as she raised her head slowly. He smiled at her. 'My dear, we'll remember that Ross is a big, strong man. He'll fight. And in that fight the healthy outdoor life he leads and his clean living will stand him in good stead. And — he has everything to live for as you know. So — how about going and having a wash and a change now? And your mother will make you a cup of tea. And later, say in a couple of hours I'll be able to get some news from the hospital and I'll come back to tell you what it is.'

'Thank you.' Bridget whispered.

'Good girl! I'll take you in to Inverness tomorrow, Bridget, to see him. I've been meaning to go in to have a look at old MacIver who is in the hospital, so we'll make it tomorrow.'

'Thank you,' Bridget murmured again. She turned away, making for the door, not looking at either her father or her mother.

Morag made as if to follow her but the doctor put out his hand to stay her. 'No, Morag,' he said. 'Let her go alone.' Morag glared at him. Alan Murray was taking too much on himself, presuming things were as they were not, encouraging Bridget. But she stood back for she did not know what she was to say to Bridget, even admitted to herself that perhaps she had gone too far.

But David after an unhappy look at his wife was asking for details and the doctor was giving them. 'Evidently they'd had a warning that something might happen somewhere in the country. Ross knew of it and so did MacPherson. They've been keeping an eye open for anyone suspicious. They must have been all ready to light their fire — and how that fire would have raged — when Ross came upon them. Then Bridget — whom I suspect was not meant to be there — arrived at the same time as the third man. MacPherson found the weapon, a piece of heavy iron piping. If he had got it on the back of his head as he would have done if Bridget had not cried out, he'd have been killed instantly.'

'He was unconscious when you got there?'

'No. I'd say he'd been fighting like hell to keep some semblance of consciousness. For Bridget was there and he'd be afraid they'd come back. When we arrived he had her crouching behind him, though what he could have done in the state he was in I don't know, poor lad.' He moved his shoulders. 'Well, I'll be off. And I'll come back as I told Bridget.'

'I'll come along to hear what you've found out if you're busy, Alan,' the minister suggested.

'No,' the doctor shook his head. 'I want to have a look at Bridget.' He gave Morag a brief nod, and moved to the door. David went with him down the path. There was something else he needed to know from his friend.

When he came back his wife had

gone into the kitchen, and he went to stand at the window, his face sombre. He swung round when Morag came back into the room. 'A very bad business, Morag,' he said quietly.

'Aye,' Morag glanced at him nervously as she set down her tray. She hesitated. 'I'd better see if Bridget is ready for her tea.'

'I'll go,' David moved but Bridget came back at that. She had washed and changed, and she looked calm after her storm of weeping. An unnatural calm, the minister thought, as he watched her sit down and accept a cup of tea from her mother with a polite Thank you. It was as if she was with strangers, to whom she must be polite, but from whom she must hide her grief, her worries.

'Alan tells me Ross knew that something might happen, Bridget.'

'Yes. That was why he had to go back this afternoon,' Bridget answered flatly. 'Last weekend too. To check that all was in order. Not that they really expected

273

anything to happen as far north as this.'
She paused, remembering what Ross
had said to her this morning. Her chin
lifted and she looked for the first time
from one to the other. 'He told me I
had to wait for him at the car. He was
adamant about that.'

'But you didn't?' David said gently.

'No.' Bridget's brows puckered. 'I
had a feeling that something was wrong
so — '

The minister nodded. That he understood. Morag cleared her throat and
asked her daughter if she would have
some more tea.

Bridget put her cup down. 'No,
thank you, Mother,' she said quietly.
'No, nothing to eat.' She got up and
walked to the window to look out. 'It
is raining now,' she said. The rain was
coming down heavily, splashing on the
garden. It would be splashing in
the forest too, washing away the
blood, hindering those who searched
for the men who had attacked Ross.
But dampening the dry twigs, the

undergrowth, the crisp leaves of those trees which Ross loved so much, which would have burned so furiously if he had not been there to save them. But — at what a cost?

10

When later that night Alan Murray came back to the manse he brought the news that Ross had survived the journey and was settled in the hospital. He was still unconscious, he was being given blood transfusions but, he told Bridget, now that the hurdle of the journey was safely over, the real treatment had begun, they could hope. Bridget had accepted that. Having so short a time before spent so long in hospital herself she knew how cautious they were about giving information and had expected no more.

'If he is still unconscious,' Mrs Sinclair said then, 'do you think it wise for Bridget to go to Inverness tomorrow, Alan?'

The doctor smiled a little grimly. Morag was nothing if not persistent. He did not know that already she was wondering if this might mean that the break between Bridget and Ledoux would come more quickly than she had hoped. For if he had to spend time in hospital, he might not even return to Achinlaig.

'We'll hope he has recovered consciousness by tomorrow afternoon,' Alan said. 'In which case he'll certainly want to see Bridget. And Bridget must see him, no matter how he is.'

'Of course,' David put in quietly, and Morag though her mouth tightened, said no more.

But the doctor had brought other news. The heavy rain, it seemed, far from hindering the search for the three men, had prevented them from getting very far away. The extra police drafted into the area, assisted by several members of the forestry team, had found them cowering under a small tent, not very far from the main road.

Bridget heard the news with a complete detachment, but for her mother it brought other thoughts. She voiced them to her husband after her daughter, having declined the doctor's offer of something to make her sleep, had agreed to have a glass of hot milk and then gone off upstairs.

'We're going to be in for some unpleasant publicity,' she said dryly.

The minister, who was trying without much success, to concentrate on the notes he had made for tomorrow's sermon, looked up. 'Publicity?'

'There'll be a trial, I suppose. Bridget will maybe need to be there.'

'Probably,' David agreed. 'From what Alan has told us it seems Bridget behaved both bravely and sensibly today, so no doubt she'll take that in her stride.'

'But it'll be in all the papers! And you know what stories they put in.'

'Well I can't see them making much of a sensational story about two straight-forward young people like Bridget and Ross. Besides, from what I read they'll be much more likely to play up the young men who've committed the offence than a mere man, who nearly loses his life for doing his duty.'

Morag hoped he was right. David watched her a moment and then gave a little sigh as he went back to his notes. Morag would have to make her own peace with her daughter for her hasty words. For, of course, she could never have meant what those words had seemed to imply. He should, and he knew it, talk to both of them about it, but could not find the right words even to begin. With his parishioners who needed or who came to him for help he was never at a loss but with his own family he was. And Bridget — unhappily he knew that both he and her mother had failed her. Bridget had withdrawn from them, and he did not know how to get through to her.

Next morning Bridget was still outwardly composed, still with that withdrawn air about her. She had slept fitfully, waking to lie worrying about Ross, wishing she could have been with him, wondering if he had regained consciousness, what news she would have of him when morning did come. And mingled with the anxiety was the bitter hurt. For Bridget had no illusions as to what her mother had meant, what her instinctive reaction had been.

It had rained heavily all night but by eight o'clock it had ceased, though the sky was still overcast. Soon after the doctor telephoned to tell Bridget he had been on to the hospital, that Ross's condition was satisfactory, he had regained consciousness during the night and was then asleep. He would call for Bridget about half past ten, he added.

'Was that Alan?' David asked as she went back into the dining room. 'How is Ross this morning, Bridget?'

Bridget answered him, telling him what the doctor had told her. The minister nodded. 'That sounds satisfactory, my dear.' He glanced at his wife. 'You must tell Ross that your mother and I are thinking of him.'

Morag nodded and Bridget looked away quickly, biting her lips to keep back the retort which she could have made. She had no intention of starting an argument with her mother about Ross.

'Shall I put you up some lunch, Bridget?' Morag asked then.

'No thank you, Mother,' Bridget said quietly. 'I'm told Aunt Janet is giving us something.'

'Janet? Is she going too?' Mrs Sinclair said hopefully. If Janet went too that would be better.

But that Bridget did not know and when the doctor's car came though Janet was with him she said she was not going with them. She had come, she told Bridget, to go with her to the hotel first, so that she could collect a few things for Ross, which he would certainly need. Bridget was grateful, both for the thought and for the implication that Ross would soon need some of his clothes.

Thay got away just before the bell in the small church started ringing for the morning service, and as it was now the

281

first day of October the road was far from busy. They had an uneventful drive in, stopping to eat their sandwiches and drink their coffee, and then going on so that they arrived at the hospital just before the afternoon's visiting was due to commence. The doctor left Bridget waiting while he went to make some enquiries, coming back in a few minutes to tell her that Ross was in a small room off one of the main wards, his condition was still satisfactory and she could go in and see him.

'He may be sleeping, Bridget. He'll be drowsy, but you'll know that. Now, my dear, I'm going to have a word with his doctor. Then I'll go and see old MacIver. I'll come and see Ross before the visiting hour is up. Now I'll show you where to go.' He took her to the end of the ward, pointing the way for her, and Bridget went on. Her heart was beating with apprehension as she opened the door of the tiny room and crossed quickly and noiselessly to the narrow bed. Ross, his dark face unbelievably pale under the white bandages had his eyes shut, he was sleeping. Bridget put down the small case she was carrying, and sat down in the chair close to the head of the bed. A smart of tears in her eyes, her throat dry, she bent over him, looking at him, putting her hands gently on top of his which rested on top of the coverlet. He stirred slightly. 'Bride,' he said and opened his eyes slowly. For a moment there was a far away look in his eyes then he smiled. 'Bridget, you're really here.'

'Yes, darling, I'm here,' Bridget bent over and kissed him. 'You called me Bride, Ross. You've never done that before,' she said unsteadily.

'No. I'm saving that,' he whispered. 'But — I was dreaming — that we were already there.' His hand under hers turned and she felt again with a swift surge of relief and hope, the tightness of his clasp. 'Bridget, are you all right?' he asked urgently. 'They didn't hurt you, touch you, did they?'

'No, no, I'm quite all right. But you — here we are talking about me and I want to know how you are.'

'Improving every minute,' Ross assured her. 'You'll have me back in Achinlaig before long. Meantime, sweetheart,' he gave her a rueful grin, 'I can't even sit up in bed without my head going round and round, and they've given me so many doses and jabs that I'm all hazy and drowsy.'

Bridget bent quickly to kiss him again. 'Oh, Ross,' she murmured, 'I was so afraid. And now, I'm so thankful.'

'I know, darling, I know. I gave you a bad time yesterday. All our plans went wrong.'

Bridget raised her head and smiled at him. 'We'll make up for it.'

'Yes.' He looked beyond her. 'How did you get here, Bridget? Who brought you?'

'Uncle Alan,' Bridget answered. 'He's away seeing old Mr MacIver who is in here too. He'll come to see you before we have to go.'

'That was good of him,' Ross said quietly. 'He came yesterday, didn't he?'

'Yes. I've brought some of your things,' she went on quickly. 'Aunt Janet went with me this morning to your room at the hotel — we thought you'd be wanting some of your clothes soon.'

'Sure I will.' He smiled. 'Right now I could do with a handkerchief. Did you bring some?'

'Yes.' Bridget got up to open the bag, glad to do something while she blinked back her tears. 'I'll put it under the pillow at the side here, Ross.'

'Thanks. I'm told everything I had on was just fit to be destroyed. And I guess I'll owe you a new outfit, sweetheart.'

Bridget smiled at him lovingly. 'Well, you're going to buy everything for me in future, aren't you?' she said in a matter-of-fact tone.

'So I am.' He smiled. 'That's a wonderful thought to hug to me.'

'Go to sleep again, Ross, if you want to.'

'No. Plenty of time to sleep later. I'm

very content as we are.'

They stayed without speaking for several minutes. 'Did you know that they'd got the three men who attacked you, Ross?' Bridget said then.

'Yes. I had a police officer in with my chief this morning. I told them what I could. What about you, Bridget?'

'I gave Sergeant MacPherson a lot of details yesterday. But Uncle Alan has arranged for him to come and see me tomorrow.'

'Your mother will be worrying in case the press starts making something of it. She won't like you to get your name in the papers,' Ross said quietly.

Bridget's change of expression was momentary, but he marked it. 'I don't know,' she said. 'I've never thought about it.'

There was a shadow in the young man's eyes. Mrs Sinclair had not approved of him before and all this, even though he could hardly be blamed, would not meet with her approval. 'You start at the bank tomorrow, Bridget.'

'Yes,' Bridget hesitated. 'I was to start. But — I thought if I came and stayed in Inverness I could come and see you each day, Ross.'

'No, don't do that, Bridget.' There was firmness in Ross's weak voice. 'You stay at home and start the job. Then you'll have less time to worry about me.' He smiled at her. 'You could only see me for a short time each day, then what would you do? I'd be worrying about you and you wouldn't want that, sweetheart.'

'No, but — ' Bridget's eyes were troubled. 'You'll seem so far away.'

'But not for long, Bridget.' He smiled. 'I'm tough. We'll write to each other every day.' His fingers tightened about her hand. 'Come closer again, darling,' he whispered and as she bent to him, putting her cheek against his, he went on, 'You know it isn't that I don't want to see you every day, Bridget, but — I don't want you to make a break at home. So — promise?'

'I know, Ross. Yes,' she agreed.

'Maybe someone will bring you in again next weekend if I'm still here.' Bridget looking at him was sure he still would be but she smiled and agreed again.

But Ross though he knew there were other things he wanted to say to her was too drowsy to concentrate properly, though he wanted to lie looking at her, was having difficulty in keeping his eyes open. After that they said little. Ross dozed for a few minutes, opened his eyes and then his heavy lids closed again. Bridget, her hand held tightly, sat quietly watching him, loving him, touching his face gently with her free hand. Several times the door opened and a nurse would look in but they were undisturbed until, about ten minutes before their precious hour would be up, Dr Murray came in.

He raised an interrogative eyebrow at Bridget. 'Is he sleeping?'

'No,' Ross opened his eyes and

answered him. 'Just floating about a bit, I guess.'

The doctor nodded and looked down at him critically. 'Well, you're in much better shape than when I saw you last, lad. No pain at present, I suppose. Not yet,' he added briskly.

Ross grinned. 'I know. I guess I can take it.' He paused and looked seriously at the other man. 'Thank you, doctor. For yesterday. And for bringing Bridget today.'

Alan smiled. 'Well, we couldn't have her trying to hitch-hike could we. We'll bring her in again, either Janet or I next Sunday, Ross, and who knows, if you're a model patient we might even be allowed to take you home with us.'

'I'll be a model patient,' Ross said earnestly. 'Doctor,' he went on, 'Bridget is starting her part-time job with Fraser tomorrow. I want her to do that.'

The doctor laughed. 'Been giving you his orders, has he, Bridget. Good sign, that. But it's a good job for you she didn't obey you yesterday, Ross.'

'I know,' Ross said deeply. His fingers gripped tighter as he glanced at Bridget. That was something between him and Bridget which he knew well did not need to be put into words. 'She is a brave girl,' he said quietly.

'She is. But I'm with you, Ross. She'll be better doing a job.' He talked to him for a few more minutes then glanced at his watch and stood up. 'Nearly time, I'm afraid, Bridget.' He gripped Ross's free hand and moved to the door, giving them the last few minutes to themselves. When Bridget joined him in the corridor he smiled at her. 'Feel better now, Bridget?'

'Yes. But — he looks so weak.'

The doctor nodded. 'Bound to, my dear. You can't lose the amount of blood he did and be fit again in a day. You and I, Bridget,' he went on solemnly, 'know it was a matter of minutes between life and death for him yesterday. But now — I'd a talk with his doctor. He's reasonably satisfied. For, of course, they've got to watch for a few days in case there are any undesirable side effects from that sort of blow. But — nothing pointing that way at present. Then they'll get him on his feet and knowing Ross he'll soon be himself again after that. Meantime you do as he says, go and do that job.'

'Yes, I will,' Bridget agreed.

'Now Janet said we had to be sure and have some tea before we started off home again, so let us go and get some.'

During the next few days Bridget was glad that she had plenty to occupy several hours of her day. Alec Fraser, always trying to do too much on his own, never able to get any reliable help, was pleased to have Bridget and delighted that she was ready to work longer than she had originally intended. On the Monday she had given a full statement to Sergeant MacPherson, each morning Dr Murray telephoned her with news from the hospital which changed from the first two days' 'Satisfactory' to 'Progressing favourably' on the Wednesday. But for the rest of the time Bridget was glad to be at the bank. For with the strained relationship at the manse she was not comfortable at home. She could not forget what her mother had said, could not think that she could ever forgive her cruel and most unjust slur on Ross.

She did not know that her mother had already forgotten what she had said, that she was coming to accept Ross Ledoux as her future son-in-law, was deciding how she would make a graceful acceptance in the eyes of the parish. That David had no doubt about it she had known on the Sunday morning when the minister had invited his congregation to join with him in praying for one of their number who was particularly close to his own family. After that public acceptance Morag had realized she would have to do likewise, and after the service had listened graciously to the murmurs of genuine sympathy. The people of Achinlaig were really shocked at what had happened in their quiet district.

That the village had closed its ranks behind the minister's family Mrs Sinclair discovered on the Monday when the manse had an unexpected caller. He had talked, she quickly gathered, to several other people in the village, but one and all had referred him to the manse. Though Bridget was at that very time working quietly in the bank, nobody apparently knew where she was. Nor when she was asked, did Morag give the information. To accept Ross into the family was one thing. To have some sensational, perhaps salacious tale, about her daughter and the young man splashed about the papers was another. She had, she was sure, dealt in a masterly fashion with the caller and sent him away with nothing on which to build such a tale. No romance, no story, she was sure. The minister was out at the time, and she did not mention the caller either to him or to Bridget.

On the Tuesday Bridget got her first letter from Ross and hoped he had got hers that morning. She read it over and over and did the same with the second which came on the Wednesday. When Thursday came she was a little later in leaving the bank and knowing that the post would already have been, hurried down to the manse. As soon as she opened the door she saw her letter lying on the hall table, but bent down first to pick up their daily paper which had apparently just been delivered. She glanced at it idly and then froze where she stood, as her own name seemed to hit her.

The inch-high letters of the headline stared back at her. 'No Romance for Bridget and the Forester,' it said and underneath 'Nonsense! says the Minister's Wife.' Bridget's face flamed as she read on quickly. She could almost hear her mother's scorn, her words, distorted and twisted even though they were with their half-truths, their omissions.

'Is that you, Bridget?' Her mother had come to the sitting room door. 'I thought I heard — ' she broke off. 'Why, what is it. Not — not — ' Somehow this time she could not say Mr Ledoux, but not yet could she say Ross.

'It is this,' Bridget said hardly and held the paper to her. Morag, taking it, changed colour as she saw that headline. And never before had she seen such scorn on her daughter's face. 'Did you really think that that would influence me, Mother?'

'Bridget, I didn't mean — I never thought — ' Mrs Sinclair began helplessly.

'No?' Bridget said icily. She moved to pick up her letter and holding it closely to her, moved quickly to the stairs and her own room. Had Ross seen that? Of course he would have done! Did he think — no, not for a moment could she think that he would think she was of the same opinion as her mother. He would be hurt even though — she could not doubt it — he already knew of her mother's disapproval. He did not and would never know what her mother had said last Saturday but — she recalled something he had said — maybe even that he guessed. He would be worried for her, for even on Sunday, dazed as he had been, he had guessed that all was not right at home. She had promised she would stay at home, go to the job, but she would not be working on Saturday. She would take the train into Inverness and stay there overnight. She would see him at least a day before she had thought to do so. She must see him, to reassure him. For when one was ill, one could have strange thoughts, fears. She knew that.

Down in the hall Mrs Sinclair was still standing gazing in horror at the newspaper in her hand. She had thought she was preventing any publicity, instead she had precipitated it. And such publicity! She shivered with shame. It was so cheap and — it made her look ridiculous. She was still standing there when David came in.

'What's wrong, Morag?' he came

quickly to her as he saw her face. Silently she handed the paper to him. His brows went up as he read it. 'Oh, Morag, Morag, how could you?' he said sadly.

'I didn't say it that way,' Mrs Sinclair said unhappily. 'I mean — I thought if I said he was just a friend of ours, there wouldn't be any story, they wouldn't put anything in. I never thought — ' She bit her lip.

'If you had just told them the truth there would have been no sensational story,' David pointed out sternly. 'Has Bridget seen this?'

Morag nodded. 'Everyone will read it.'

'Everyone. Including Ross.'

Mrs Sinclair blanched. That had not occurred to her. 'Maybe he doesn't get this paper.'

'Well, if he doesn't someone will show it to him,' David said tersely. He frowned. 'I'd better write to him, I think. Try to explain.' He glanced at the clock. It was too late now to catch the day's post. Ross would not get any letter now till Saturday morning. 'And I'd better have a word with Bridget.'

But Bridget met her father's explanation that her mother had not meant what she had seemed to mean, that she had been flustered when confronted by a reporter and given him the wrong impression, with a cool 'No? All she had to do was tell the truth. I hardly think that would have made a sensational story.'

The minister, who was of the same opinion, had left it. And Mrs Sinclair, still aghast at what she had done and knowing — and the one person whose opinion she valued above all was her husband — that David was deeply displeased with her, had nothing to say. She did not know how she was to face anyone, her friends, all the people of the village. When Friday came, though on that day she usually went down to the store, she did not go. She could not face people. She hoped no one came to the manse. But midway in the afternoon she heard the knock at the front door and started nervously. Bridget was not back yet; David was in his study. Who could it be? It might even be another reporter.

She opened the door and for once lost all her colour as she stared. Ross Ledoux looked at big as ever, as dark as ever, but his face had a pallor it had never had, and his head was still bandaged. 'Good afternoon, Mrs Sinclair,' he said quietly, but he did not smile.

'Why — why — how are — ' Morag gulped. 'Bridget isn't here.'

'No. Is Mr Sinclair at home? May I see him?'

'Of course.' She backed up. 'Come in.'

But the minister had heard and he was coming quickly across the hall. 'Ross! What are you doing here? Ought you to be out of hospital?'

'There is something I have to do, so I came,' Ross said simply.

David frowned. 'How did you get here? Has someone brought you?'

'I came on the train and the bus. May I see you for a few minutes, Mr Sinclair?'

'Of course, Ross. Come in here and sit down.' The minister looked meaningly at his wife.

'I'll make some tea,' she murmured and moved to the kitchen door.

Ross paused. 'No. Could you wait, Mrs Sinclair, please. For this concerns you too.' He stood aside for her to go into the room before him, and she went and sat down, looking at him with a mixture of nervousness, for she did not know what he was going to say to her, and of compassion, for that he should not be here was obvious.

'Sit down, Ross,' David said.

Ross shook his head. 'I'll stand,' he said quietly, but both noticed that he had to take hold of the back of a chair to steady himself. But he held himself erect as he faced them. 'This is something that Bridget and I had intended to do together last Saturday but — we were prevented. I had thought I'd made it very clear but yesterday I realized that I had not, that I had to put the record straight immediately. Bridget and I intend to get married.'

'Of course you do, Ross,' the minister said quickly. 'We,' he put a slight emphasis on the word, 'know that.'

Ross gave Mrs Sinclair a brief glance and looked back at David. 'We intend to get married at the end of this month,' he went on firmly. 'As I think you know I finish in Achinlaig then. So — '

'You are going back to Canada then, Ross?' David said gently.

'No. Not till next April. I want Bridget to start with a spring and a summer, instead of a winter.' Ross went on, 'They've asked me to do a further six months over here, so I've taken them up on that. I'm to be stationed near Kyle, and there is a small house we can have. So we've decided — ' He looked straightly at the minister. 'I want Bridget to stay in her home until she is married. I hope, sir, that you will marry us.'

David started. But could he blame them? He smiled at the younger man. 'Ross, I have every intention of doing that.'

'Thank you,' Ross said quietly and looked at Morag. She gave her husband a nervous look and moistened her lips with her tongue. 'The end of the month you say?' she said.

'Yes. I have some leave due. And — my parents will come over to see us married. That will give them time to make arrangements.'

'Will they?' Morag looked at him, seeing him in a way she had not done before. 'They will be surprised.'

For the first time Ross smiled. 'I doubt it. As my letters home have been full of Bridget since the beginning — ' He looked at her straightly. 'Mrs Sinclair, I know I'm not what you wanted for Bridget. But — ' he went on with deep sincerity, 'to me she is — everything in the world. And,' his chin lifted. This was no time for false modesty and he knew it, 'that is what I am to her.'

Morag had coloured at his first direct words. Now she groped for what she should say, what she ought to say. But before she could say anything they heard the front door open and than a running step across the hall. Ross swung round and opened his arms and Bridget went into them, holding him, burying her face on his shoulder. Morag, staring, perhaps for the first time realized that her daughter was not a pale shadow of herself, content to be always that, but a woman who had chosen her own life, her own man. She caught the look on Ross Ledoux's face as he looked down at Bridget, as he held her closely in his arms, and looked away quickly, embarrassed. She stood up.

'I'll away and make some tea,' she said briskly. 'I'm sure Ross could do with some.'

David, as he followed her, rested his

hand briefly on the young man's shoulder as he passed him, and shut the door behind them. In the kitchen Morag turned to him. 'I'll tell him I was wrong. I'll apologize to him, David,' she said breathlessly.

The minister smiled at her gently. 'He won't expect that of you, Morag. He is — a big man.'

'Yes.' Perhaps Morag's look was a little uncertain. 'The end of the month, he says. There will be a lot to do.' Already she was planning, deciding what she would say in the village. 'We'll give her a real nice wedding, David. Something for them to remember when they go to Canada. Won't we?'

'Of course, Morag. You and Bridget decide just what you want. I'm sure,' he smiled again, 'I'll be able to afford it.'

In the sitting room Bridget had raised her head. 'Ross, you shouldn't be here. What did you do, just walk out?' she asked anxiously.

Ross smiled at her lovingly. 'Shall we say I persuaded them. I've to go back next week for a check. Meantime I'm to put myself in Dr Murray's hands. No doubt you'll see I do that.'

'Yes.' Bridget's eyes were troubled as she looked up at him. 'Ross, you read the newspaper?'

'Yes. I realized there was something that needed doing. That there was a misunderstanding. So I had to come to put the record right. I've told them now, sweetheart. They know. Everything is all fixed.

'I was coming tomorrow, Ross. I was going to stay. I thought, perhaps I'd stay on and not come back.'

'I was afraid of that,' Ross said solemnly. 'You know I didn't want that. But it doesn't matter now. We'll forget it.'

'Forget?' Bridget said doubtfully.

'Yes,' Ross said firmly. 'I expect she got a bit confused when they started throwing questions at her.' He bent his head and rested his cheek briefly against hers. 'And somewhere along the line I went wrong. I don't know where but I must have done. I wanted everyone to know from the first what I meant, I wanted everything to be perfect for you, nothing was to mar your courtship.' He shook his head slightly at himself. 'I was optimistic. I even, because of my calling,' he went on solemnly, 'had to lead you into a situation in which in your sort of life, you should never have been.'

'You couldn't control that,' Bridget said quickly. 'And where else should I have been if not with you when you were in danger.' She put her hand up and touched his face. 'Ross,' she went on earnestly, 'loving, as we mean it, is sharing. Not only all the wonderful, joyful things as we do, we are going to share. But the sad, the unpleasant, the difficult things too.' She smiled at him. 'I don't think anyone can protect another from those. But — I expect you'll go on trying to do it.'

'You'll have to let me do that.' He bent then, touching her mouth with his, and they kissed each other slowly and

A KISS IN TANGIER

Denise Conway

Flying to Tangier to look after five-year-old Tommy is more complicated than Eve had expected: Dean, a widower, is an indifferent father, and his Arab housekeeper sinister. Puzzled and uneasy, Eve turns to Evan, a young man who assisted her before. However, when Nadia arrives Eve realises that her new-found love is doomed, although she is too entangled in the web of intrigue to leave. And when danger threatens, her only thought is to help the man she loves.

THE STOLEN IMAGE

Elaine Daniel

Alexei Baran is the notoriously difficult, publicity-shy star of the Imperial Ballet. On the strength of her previous pictures of him Anna, a photographer, is asked to portray the ballet company at work. Almost in self-defence she becomes engaged to James Farmer, but this proves to be no protection at all against falling in love with Baran. But when he discovers how she has used his captured image, Alexei is determined that she should steal no more of him . . .